A week on the road with a general's daughter . . .

Dev's eyes became narrow slits as he studied Pepper. A week with her, shut in that frivolous, flashy little car would be about six days too many. He glanced distastefully at the lunging, barking sheepdog whose collar she clutched.

"Where's this dog going?" Dev shifted his bag to the other hand. "And I use the term *dog* loosely."

"With us, Major. The dog is headed for his owner in Sierra Vista. Right on our way."

"Two adults and a mutt crammed in a sardine can? No way," Dev declared hotly. "Anyway, dogs don't take to me."

"I can understand that." Pepper smirked broadly as she led Smedley to the open car door. "Well, perhaps you'd like to call your father and tell him you've changed your mind. Smedley was invited first." *So it wasn't quite the truth . . .*

Before she could blink, Dev had tossed his pack and duffle in on top of hers. "I just bet you'd like me to do that. Well, forget it, lady, because I intend to figure out what little scheme our families have hatched by the time we reach Arizona."

Roz Denny has lived all over the United States, including, of course, the Southwest, so vividly described in *Red Hot Pepper*. Some of the other locales she and her family have experienced will likely find their way into future Romances!

Red Hot
Pepper

Roz Denny

Harlequin Books

TORONTO • NEW YORK • LONDON
AMSTERDAM • PARIS • SYDNEY • HAMBURG
STOCKHOLM • ATHENS • TOKYO • MILAN

ISBN 0-373-03032-0

Harlequin Romance first edition February 1990

CHAPTER ONE

Rrring.

"Wade, it's T. Bird Huston here. You deserve to know why I'm packin' Devlin off to Raul's post. He's a bright boy, Wyndom. Just too darn popular with the ladies. Find him a wife, Win—that's an order."

Slam. Click.

PEPPER RIVERA WRIGGLED her right foot out of one red leather high-heeled shoe and with an audible sigh of relief touched her bare toe cautiously to the gas pedal of her new sports car. The Ferrari, whose sleek finish was only a shade more scarlet than her too snug shoes, responded powerfully, giving Pepper the same sense of liberation she'd felt in the welcome release from her confining shoe. She slowed the car just long enough to ease her foot out of the other one.

So this was what freedom felt like! The idea brought a spontaneous smile to her lips. She could almost hear the lecture this small act of rebellion would have elicited from her father, General Raul Rivera. Picturing Papa's favorite reproving look prompted another impulsive smile of satisfaction.

At the side of the road, a signpost appeared briefly, then faded away behind her as the Ferrari skimmed over the flat ribbon of west Texas highway. Pepper rapidly calculated the number of miles she had yet to travel before arriving at her final destination—the massive army base of Fort Bliss.

Despite the lateness of the hour, her calculations showed she could make the base in enough time to keep the appointment with her Papa's old army buddy, General Wyndom Wade. Flexing her unfettered toes in the car's thick carpet, Pepper smiled again, a smile of pure pleasure that stemmed from the exhilaration of commanding a fast car over an open road.

Still, there was a decided relief in knowing she wouldn't be late, considering the argument she and Papa had had earlier when he discovered that she intended to make this trip alone, unchaperoned. Even recalling it brought a return of righteous indignation over the way he persisted in treating her as though she were fifteen rather than the twenty-five she'd turned today.

But all things being relative, it had been a minor skirmish compared to the series of major battles she and Papa had been having of late. Not a single one of his arguments had induced Pepper to find herself a husband—"to take care of her"—which was what the autocratic general insisted his daughter needed.

Smoldering from the memory, Pepper popped the sunroof in search of a breath of air. What she resented most was not the way Papa handed down orders, because he was trained to give orders, after all, but the way her older brothers were now getting into the act. Lately, the entire Rivera family, except Pete who'd just returned from a tour of duty abroad, seemed to be meddling in her life.

Sailing around a tight curve, the Ferrari bore down suddenly on a big dark Ford. Pepper was practically on top of the black car before she realized it was a military vehicle—a staff car, complete with a lone passenger in the back seat. *Probably another officer good at giving orders,* she thought spitefully. *The way they all are.*

Pausing for another look at her watch, she whisked around the older car, still on time. At least she could feel reassured her overprotective father wouldn't be calling out the militia to find her. Seeking any small respite from the summer sun, Pepper unfastened the top two buttons of her dress, ignoring the staff car as it overtook and passed her.

Almost absently, she noted the corporal's stripes on the olive-drab sleeve of the staff vehicle's youthful driver and registered his flirtatious half-salute.

Dismissing the corporal's covert wave as no more than admiration for her car, Pepper removed her sunglasses and squinted into a fireball sun, transferring all her attention to the dials on the Ferrari's air conditioner. Repeated adjustments gave absolutely no relief from the blistering heat. And to think, she lamented in disgust, she'd given that man at the last service center fifty dollars and one hour of her time to diagnose the unit's ailment. She should have saved both time and money and prevailed on her brother Pete to fix it later.

Pepper suddenly slammed on her brakes, realizing that she'd once again caught up to the dark sedan. This time she observed that the officer seated in back was raven haired—and rather young to be in command of a staff car. All the more reason, Pepper thought, to indulge in a moment of irritation. She even begrudged him the air-conditioned government car that allowed him to look so cool and aloof.

Frowning, she pulled around them. Young officers were something else she and Papa had been squabbling about lately. His constant parade of what he termed "suitable husband material" had started when he and Grandmother Rivera deemed it to be long past the proper time for a woman Pepper's age to be married.

Then Pepper got a quick glimpse of the posted speed limit and she slowed down. The old staff car moved up behind her again. Catching her eye in the rearview mirror, the corporal flashed her a clear-cut invitation to race.

Pepper laughed out loud. Whatever would the spit-and-polish officer, who seemed totally oblivious to his driver's actions, say if he discovered the soldier was hankering to take on her Ferrari? Her laugh mellowed until it was nothing more than an impish grin.

IN THE AIR-CONDITIONED staff car, Major Devlin Wade paid scant attention to the merciless sun or the sports car up ahead. His thoughts were on his new orders, spread across the rear seat of the vehicle that his father had sent to fetch him.

He glanced once at Corporal Farron Roberts and caught the driver studying him in the mirror with interest. Had scuttlebutt concerning his recent fall from grace at the Pentagon already reached Fort Bliss? Devlin wondered disgustedly. Was the corporal measuring him against his reputation as the major who had a way with women—particularly a certain general's wife?

Lips pressed in a tight line, the major turned away and chanced to glimpse the sleek, red Ferrari through his side window. He knew the car from its advertising campaign. A top-of-the-line Italian import, designed to make a man's blood boil.

Wade thought his own blood was more conservative. Given a choice, he'd take a dove-gray Mercedes with wine leather interior any day. Or at least he would any day except today. Today, he had more to ponder than luxury cars. For months now he'd been planning to resign his commission. A plan that had been taking shape since the morning he'd looked in the mirror and decided that thirty-two was too old to be facing ten more years of taking endless orders. Too old for another ten long years of nomadic life. What he wanted, he'd decided, was to be free to put down roots, free to operate the little wine shop he'd purchased in Alexandria, and he wanted time to renovate the old Virginia farmhouse he'd had his eye on.

In spite of the fact that he had more crucial things to think about, his mind kept wandering. Still, Devlin was not blind to Corporal Roberts's indiscretion. For the moment, the corporal's fun looked harmless enough. However, Dev knew that very soon he'd have to speak up and call a halt.

Roberts passed the sports car again and this time cut a shade too sharply in front. Dev snatched at papers sliding across the back seat and lost his sunglasses in the process.

His head swiveled to the rear. Unconsciously Dev held his breath as the driver of the crimson power-plant backed off the gas, barely avoiding a collision. The smaller car still hovered much too close to the Ford's bumper to suit Dev. Slowly he released his breath, a reprimand ready on the tip of his tongue. It was then, for the first time, that he really saw the driver of the Ferrari, and knew why the corporal was showing off.

Shimmering copper-colored tresses drifting through the sports car's sunroof captured Dev's attention, further delaying his rebuke. For a tense moment, his gaze followed the thready strands of red-gold, dancing hypnotically in the dazzle of the Texas sun. And still the lady seemed unaware of how close her bumper rode, nose to trunk behind his car. He stayed motionless for a few seconds, studying porcelain cheeks curving gently into a slender throat—and below, where a hint of creamy skin peeked from beneath a snug-fitting garment, as red as the car she drove.

As Dev leisurely completed his survey, a faint derisive smile tugged at one corner of his lips. Apparently Corporal Roberts had a lot to learn of mice and women, he thought, amused. Someone really should tell the kid that the more tempting the cheese, the more lethal the trap.

Just then, the tantalizing redhead lifted her lashes and caught him staring. Devlin swallowed hard, galvanized by an unfamiliar flicker of beguiling innocence. But as the lady grew aware of being studied, her chin tilted and she shot him a frosty glare. Dev uttered a mirthless laugh, disappointed at finding her typical, after all, in the way she pretended to be insulted by his harmless inspection. Well, she needn't worry about him, he thought, gnashing his teeth. He'd sworn off women.

Turning abruptly, Dev faced the front, wanting—no, needing—to demand that Roberts give up this silly game. Yet surprisingly, his voice lay tangled in the tightness of his throat. He took a moment to focus on an endless blur of sagebrush and heat devils sizzling in the distance, a blur broken only by the slow rhythmic nod of pumping oil rigs.

In Washington, it was a woman who had been at the bottom of this sudden and unwelcome change in his life. Her innocent-looking face was still much too vivid for him to feel favorably inclined toward any other woman. Dev replaced his sunglasses with cool deliberation, waiting for his pulse to slow, matching the lazy rigs.

All at once the Ferrari shot around them on the left, blocking Devlin's view. A red streak whistled close to his window followed by a long loud horn blast echoing inside the old sedan. And inside his head.

Losing control of the car, the corporal jerked the steering wheel sharply to the right. For less than a heartbeat the ungainly Ford tilted crazily in midair, then careered off the asphalt, spinning its wheels in deep sand.

Dev grabbed wildly for the attaché case ripped violently from his loose grasp. The rear of the sedan fishtailed giddily before shuddering to a halt, half-in, half-out of an arroyo. Dust and tumbleweeds rose in a thick cloud, hung in the air, then slowly settled around them.

Throwing open the door, Dev leaped from the car only to catch a fleeting glimpse of the sun's rays bouncing erratically off the polished rear of the red Ferrari as it sped into the distance.

"Damn," Dev swore, raking a hand through damp hair beginning to curl over scowling black brows. "I didn't even get her license number. Damn it all!"

"Red Hot," mumbled Corporal Roberts, bending to retrieve his dark glasses, which the rough ride had thrown to the floor. Straightening, he set them carefully on an ashen face.

"I wasn't asking for your opinion of her wheels or my mood, Corporal," Wade snapped back. "Did you get her license number?"

"Red Hot," repeated Roberts dazedly. Then as if realizing who was asking, he scrambled from the car, held the major's door open wider and stood at attention, chin tucked tight against his chest. "I mean Red Hot, sir! That's what it said on her license plate, sir."

"At ease, Corporal." Dev stuffed papers carelessly into his attaché case, then shaded his eyes to scan the horizon. Barbed wire followed the line of the road, leaving a quarter-mile of barren desert between highway and oil pumps. There was no other movement anywhere that Wade could see. He was left with a vague uneasiness that the Ferrari had been a mirage.

Farron Roberts hunkered down to look at the underpinnings of the old Ford. "This road doesn't go anywhere but Fort Bliss, Major. Most of the Fort's out on tactical maneuvers this week. Unless a tank rolls by, ain't likely to see much traffic here."

Dev dropped to his haunches beside the driver. "You mean that Ferrari belongs to some army brat? I'll have her daddy's stripes for this."

Roberts wiped sweat and an indulgently wry grin from his face with a broad white handkerchief. "Plates were outta' Arizona, Major. Nobody here has a set of wheels like that."

"Come on, Corporal. Fort Bliss is a big post."

Roberts straightened to stand loosely. "Beggin' your pardon, sir...the only person on this post well-heeled enough to afford that car is your father."

Wade's lips twitched. He supposed it was natural that the corporal would know of his relationship to the polished general the troops called Gentleman Win. But he would have been happier if it wasn't commonly known that he was visiting the crusty general before reporting to his forced duty station, Fort Huachuca, Arizona. Dev stiffened involuntarily. The base of his exile was properly pronounced Wa-choo-ka, which sounded like nothing so much as a sneeze to his eastern ears. And to his urban way of thinking, the place itself was situated in the back of beyond.

In short, Dev Wade didn't think his new duty station had anything to recommend it. But then, how much did the corporal, or for that matter, Gentleman Win himself, know about his exile? Would rumor-mongers have passed along information about a certain counterpart at the Pentagon coveting his next promotion? Did they know there was

strong evidence he'd been set up—framed—because he'd
unwisely befriended the young and lonely wife of a four-star
general, Thurmond Huston?

Dev unconsciously ground his teeth. He hadn't even put
in for the damn promotion, and friendship was all he'd ever
offered Candy Huston. Though he might not like the pomp
and circumstance of military protocol, he did consider
himself an honorable man. Married spelled taboo, plain and
simple. For that reason, if no other, Dev felt righteously in-
dignant over this shuffle. Grim-faced, he returned to the car
and motioned the corporal to do the same.

In total silence, Roberts jockeyed the car onto the road.
Then he cleared his throat and muttered, "I'm probably as
much to blame for this as the lady, sir." His tone reflected a
reluctant mixture of chagrin and respect.

Wade's glittering gaze raked the dusty landscape. This
was the last place he wanted to be, yet how could he in good
conscience blame the youthful driver for this seething rest-
lessness he was feeling?

Even now he should be breaking the news to Gentleman
Win. A very long line of General Wades was about to end.
He knew the general would be furious and wouldn't put it
past the Old Man to have him court-martialed on some
trumped-up charge—like this accident. Inasmuch as the
driver of the flashy Ferrari was really at fault here, she might
as well keep him company in the stockade.

"Stop at the gate, Corporal," Devlin said tightly. "We'll
see how fast the M.P.'s cool your red hot mama."

SEVERAL MILES slid away before Pepper slowed the Ferrari
and considered turning back to help the men. She kept one
eye glued to the rearview mirror, expecting any moment to
see the black car reappear. The military vehicle was big and
heavy, she reasoned, so a little bouncing around shouldn't
have hurt it. Neither of the men had looked injured, or she
would have stopped. Surely two able-bodied men could
handle the situation. Besides, if she turned back now,

General Wade would be kept waiting. But why, when technically it was not her fault, did she feel so guilty?

"I'm not," she argued, green eyes flashing back at her from the car mirror. "The officer in that car was smirking. Eating a little dust will serve him right."

Pepper couldn't bring herself to criticize the corporal for his interest in the Ferrari. At his age, any one of her brothers would have done the same. In fact she expected to see Pete drooling over the car when she met him later today. Unless being newly promoted to captain had changed Pete, too. Pepper made a face. The dark-haired officer back there had looked positively satisfied when his driver cut her off. He should have acted more professionally.

"Lord," she said with a laugh, wrinkling her freckle-splattered nose and talking aloud to her mirror image. "Listen to you, Mary Kathleen Angelina Rivera. Since when have you become a saint?"

Pepper glanced ruefully at her reflection. She'd been tagged with the nickname Pepper when her oldest brother, Ruben, joked that she was three parts red chili pepper, one part hellion. Maybe she would have been different if her mother hadn't died so young. Or maybe if her hair was straight and black like the Rivera side of the family, instead of flame red, a legacy of her mother's Scottish heritage, she wouldn't have found it so hard to conform. But she was Raul Rivera's daughter as much as she'd been Maggie McTavish's. And although she wanted to, she hadn't yet kicked over the traces, hadn't yet left the home where it was acceptable for a girl to marry at sixteen, but not for a woman to live alone at twenty-five.

Pepper tromped on the gas and felt the wind sift her hair as the Ferrari unwound with a high-pitched whine. This car represented her bid for freedom, bought after Papa prevented her from moving into an apartment of her own as most women her age did. The entire Rivera clan, steeped in generations of patriarchal rule, wouldn't hear of her moving out until she was married. And loving her father and five older brothers as she did, she had only ever dared small demonstrations of rebellion. Yet neither her family nor Sister Xavier at Saint Bernadette's Academy had succeeded in totally thwarting a streak of independence.

Pepper addressed her reflection with a seriousness that belied her untamed look. Better to concentrate on the upcoming appointment with General Wade, she told herself. It made no difference that he was an old friend of her father's. The man had never set eyes on her before, and he was the cornerstone of her latest plan. She needed to make a good first impression.

Perhaps if she could sell General Wade on the idea of this cot, Papa would see her as a real inventor. Perhaps he and Ruben would quit making decisions for "poor little Pepper" and lay off dragging home every eligible bachelor in the southwestern States and northern Mexico as a candidate for marriage.

Pepper smiled, a bit smugly. Papa indulged her "inventor fantasies," but he wouldn't hear of her getting a regular job, though he often bragged to others about her cleverness. Her smile slipped as she remembered how upset he'd been when the army bought her very first invention—a lightweight canteen with a collapsible inner core.

She patted the wood-grained steering wheel. He'd been borderline furious when her last "little whim," silent snaps for backpacks, produced enough money to buy the Ferrari. She felt her smile fade, remembering the terrible row that had followed.

Now an entirely new invention was bringing her to Fort Bliss and General Wade. A portable cot, strong enough to hold the heaviest of soldiers, yet easily collapsible, folded tube inside tube until it was no bigger than a flashlight. If she could sell the army on this idea, she might convince her family that she had the wherewithal to live alone. And General Wyndom Wade controlled the committee behind the bidding process.

Pepper gripped the steering wheel with renewed determination. She'd give it her best shot, and after that she would put her hopes and plans aside and spend two glorious days vacationing with Pete. She'd even treat him to dinner tonight if he promised to fix the Ferrari's air conditioner. There would be time enough later to worry about returning home to Papa's meddlesome matchmaking.

Approaching the entrance to Fort Bliss, Pepper slowed the Ferrari to a crawl and mustered a warm smile for the baby-faced private as she offered him her dependent's I.D. card.

"Help you, miss?" The young soldier smiled back as he stepped up to greet her.

She watched the boy admire her car, accepting his appreciation of the Ferrari as her due.

Nearly dropping her identification, he motioned to someone inside the guard shack. Two military police of higher rank stepped out, unabashedly curious. One approached, examining her I.D.

Pepper studied a billboard map of the post as she waited for the private to return. She didn't mean to let her eye trace the heavy black line marking the highway, or to estimate the location of her recent encounter with a staff car.

Was it possible that she'd simply overreacted to the whole incident? Maybe she'd misinterpreted the man's intention. It wouldn't be the first time she'd viewed an officer with a jaundiced eye. Besides, what if the staff car had suffered damage? Then it would be her responsibility to see to it that they received help, wouldn't it?

One of the M.P.'s walked over, leaned down and handed back her card. "Nice car," he said offhandedly.

Before Pepper knew it, she'd blurted out her story, and ended by describing the staff car's plight. All three M.P.'s began to shoot questions at her. One made notes. As the questions grew more detailed and faster, the more animated Pepper's tale became. She suddenly wondered whether she'd made a mistake in saying anything at all about the incident.

"Oh, no!" she exclaimed, catching sight of the time. "Listen, why don't we just forget it? I'll be late for my appointment."

"Carry on, Miss Rivera," the serious lieutenant told her, closing his note pad with a snap. "You've given us plenty to go on. Don't you worry about a thing. We'll handle it. We hope you have a pleasant stay at Fort Bliss, ma'am."

Pepper returned his smile with some misgivings. As she drove away, she couldn't help feeling that she might have given them the wrong impression. The blame, it seemed to her, was being squarely placed on the ranking officer in the staff car.

After parking in front of General Wade's office, Pepper tugged on her shoes, straightened her dress and did up the top three buttons as she mulled over this new dilemma.

It wasn't as if she'd asked to have the officer and his driver beheaded. On the contrary, she'd acted from unselfish motives—she hadn't wanted to leave them stranded on that hot Texas highway. Chewing at her bottom lip, she gathered up her cost estimates and a prototype of the cot. With one last hasty appraisal of her appearance, Pepper entered General Wade's office, promising herself she'd return to the guard shack later to straighten out any misunderstanding.

A charming, middle-aged secretary presented Pepper, and tall, courtly General Wade welcomed her into his regimented, teak-paneled office. "How is Raul getting on, Mary Kathleen? Or perhaps you would rather I called you Mary Kate?"

"Papa sends his best, General Wade." Pepper eyed him speculatively. "You may call me Mary Kate if you like, though everyone usually calls me Pepper." She gave a casual shrug.

General Wade studied her a moment. Nodding, he acknowledged the information, yet Pepper noticed he didn't offer to use her nickname. Soon any thought of the earlier incident was pushed to the back of her mind. General Wade might be an old friend of her father's, but he was also a hard-headed businessman.

Pepper made her presentation in a straightforward manner, listing the advantages of her design. "So you see,

General," she concluded, "my cot is multifaceted—useful in either barracks or bivouac. I've been told the army is looking to replace all the old cots eventually. I think you'll find mine a cost-effective alternative." Reaching for a dark-green cylinder, she said, "Here, let me demonstrate how easy this is to assemble. Then you can test its sturdy structure."

"That's the cot? All of it?" General Wade studied the plastic tube with obvious doubt. Behind him, the telephone shrilled, cutting off further comment.

"Please excuse me, Mary Kate." His tone was formal. "Go ahead, assemble."

Jerking up the receiver he answered gruffly, "Madelyn, I thought I asked you to hold my calls. Oh . . . yes. Well, put him on."

Pepper saw his brows draw together in a tight frown. He closed his eyes and pinched the bridge of his nose between thumb and forefinger the way her father did when he was forced to deal with an unpleasant task. She worked quickly and quietly, wondering if she should leave.

"Lyons, what in thunder is going on down there? Why have you detained Devlin?" The General's voice was harsh, and Pepper felt relieved not to be on the receiving end of that demand.

General Wade raked one hand through a short shock of gray hair. "He did what?" The general's yelp made Pepper jump. "When?" His last terse question brought her startled green eyes up to meet his glittering cobalt ones.

"I see," he said, holding her gaze. "Yes, yes. Damn right he's old enough to know better."

Pepper watched his shoulders slump. It reminded her of how her father looked each time Miguel had a run-in at college. But there was always hope. Her brother was a county sheriff now.

"No, Lyons, I don't know what's going on inside Dev's head, but I damn sure intend to find out. Send him over, will you? I'll get to the bottom of this."

Pepper dropped her gaze to the webbed netting of the cot. Whatever was bothering General Wade didn't concern her.

"And Lyons," he continued, "thanks for calling me first. I appreciate your being discreet." Quietly he replaced the receiver. For a long moment General Wade sat, silent and motionless, contemplating the telephone. As he passed a hand over his mouth and chin, Pepper detected a slight tremble.

"Is anything wrong, General?" Her soft question pulled him from his reverie.

"Remind me to ask Raul someday how he managed to raise six of you singlehanded."

She laughed, a low, melodic chuckle. "He's like a mother hen, that's how. But he's signed over worry of Ruben, Miguel and Manuel to their wives. I suspect if he ever succeeds in getting Pete and me married off, he'll have avoided a nervous breakdown."

"Marriage... Marriage... Yes! T. Bird Huston suggested that."

Pepper stopped smiling. General Wade jumped to his feet and began pacing the room. He was making her nervous. Each time he passed by, he paused to stare intently at her before he resumed pacing.

She cleared her throat. "General...the cot is ready. How would you like to try it out? You'll see what I mean about its comfort."

"Cot?" he repeated tonelessly. "Oh, yes."

For a moment, Pepper wondered if there was something wrong with General Wade. Maybe he had a war injury that Papa had neglected to tell her about.

He stopped pacing and sat down heavily. The cot's webbing dropped but didn't touch the floor. "Come, Mary Kate." He patted the place at his side. "Sit down here and tell me how Raul managed to arrange suitable marriages for his sons. It takes a special kind of woman to marry an army man."

Pepper did as she was asked, trying not to show her distaste for the word *arrange*. "I'm sure it does, General. However none of my married brothers is in the military."

The blue eyes now level with hers narrowed disheartingly. Pepper's tender heart melted, reaching out to him. Gentleman Win must indeed have a serious problem concerning one of his children, she decided. Pepper knew very little about this man, except that General Wade was an old respected friend of her father's, and a fellow Catholic.

Suddenly, before she could offer sympathy, the door to the General's office flew inward. It slammed against the wall, rattling the coat of arms hanging there, and creaked menacingly on its hinges.

Both occupants seated on the cot jumped, turning as one to face the noise.

Pepper's shocked gaze started at a pair of gleaming black shoes and slowly traveled up long, Sunday-creased trousers, passing lean hips and a broad torso before coming to rest on the iciest blue eyes she'd ever seen. She tried to concentrate on the shifting coat of arms, but found it made her dizzy. And the disapproving azure eyes beneath straight black brows looked somehow familiar.

"General?" Devlin Wade's chilly question exploded into the room. His eyebrow arched, meeting a thatch of wind-whipped curls. In one deft motion, he slammed the door and spun on his heel, glaring at his father. This time the family crest threatened to fall.

"Devlin!" General Wade struggled to stand. Pepper offered a hand to steady him. All at once recognition dawned, and the room, like the heavy crest, tilted dangerously. Again she let her gaze travel the length of the man, almost feeling the tense muscles trapped beneath the expertly tailored shirt. A shirt of military green.

Her eyes widening, Pepper focused on a row of medals prominently displayed on his left shoulder...and a gold oak leaf above a name tag she was too far away to read. *It was the officer from the staff car.* Her pulse slowed and her interest waned. In Pepper's rating book of men, officers were one step up from Lucifer. And the way this particular major exuded all that tense and predatory virility, he might well be one step down.

The general broke the extended moment of silence. "I didn't expect you so soon, my boy."

"That's obvious," came Devlin's clipped reply. Though he met his father's outstretched hand, his glittering gaze didn't leave the woman still seated on the net contraption. With a sinking feeling, Dev realized they'd already met. Well, not really met. He'd only glimpsed her from a moving car. How could he have been so blind as to think this woman was an army brat?

If ever the devil wore skirts, this femme fatale in the scarlet dress was surely it. Her eyes, transparent as Circe's sea, were equally dangerous. Those same guileless eyes had certainly worked to charm the M.P.'s back at the gate, Dev thought, letting his anger rise along with a memory of innocent-looking Candy Huston. Glaring down, he muttered through clenched teeth, "You have some nerve setting the M.P.'s on me, lady. You ran *my* car off the road."

Pepper stared, the heat of physical attraction only just beginning to recede. Still, she jumped to her feet, reacting to his unwarranted accusation. Adept at defending herself against five opinionated brothers, she replied with an alacrity that was second nature. "Your driver cut me off. I almost landed in your trunk. You had some nerve yourself, allowing that."

General Wade settled against his desk. Slowly, his gaze shifted from one to the other, and despite her annoyance, Pepper noticed that he wasn't stopping this rude, interfering officer from breaking the rules.

Devlin snorted ungraciously, ignoring his father's rank. "So Corporal Roberts misjudged how fast the old Ford would go. Hardly a good reason to have us zapped at the gate."

"I did no such thing!" Pepper disputed, piously recalling her earlier concern. "Not that your actions—your leering—wouldn't have deserved it, anyhow." Leaning toward him, hands on hips, Pepper matched him glare for glare. Then she pulled back, horrified at finding herself and the major squabbling like two children, and in General Wade's presence, too.

Dev's lip curled. "Since when is looking against the law? Where I've been living, people who advertise in red—red car, red hair, red dress," he said with soft menace, "quite frankly ask to be leered at. And more." Provocatively, and despite the fact that his father was looking on, Dev brushed an index finger lightly across the top button on Pepper's dress. A button that earlier had been undone. His fingers itched to unbutton it again. *Was he crazy?* The finger touching the button trembled.

Pepper forgot all about the general, drawing her breath in on a hiss. She slapped his finger away sharply, knowing he couldn't miss her embarrassment. She felt her angry flush deepen as General Wade's harsh command sliced through air thick with tension.

"Ten-hut." His rolling command echoed, bringing Pepper's head around. Dev threw his father an angry scowl, then automatically his heels came together with a click. His shoulders formed a perfect parallel to the floor.

"Sir," he answered with a brusque salute. Devlin's tightly controlled anger was evidenced by the taut lines of his mouth and the icy glitter in his blue eyes. During his career, the general had routinely manipulated him, but had never outright pulled rank on him before. Still smarting from his transfer—and the reasons for it—not to mention the indignity of being questioned at the gate, Dev switched all his irritation toward the impudent redhead.

Holding his son at attention, General Wade turned, focusing on Pepper. She saw his eyes soften and supposed there had been enough byplay for him to judge what had happened.

"My wife is having a dinner party at the house tonight, Mary Kate. As you can see I have a small matter of insubordination to deal with first." Gentleman Win smiled, spreading his palms in apology. "Bring the cot. We'll discuss it more tonight."

Pepper bent and quickly began to dismantle the cot. Tonight she had planned a reunion dinner with Pete. And yet the whole purpose of this trip was to sell General Wade on her idea.

"I wouldn't want to disrupt your party, sir." She was surprised how calm her voice sounded, as her fingers were shaking. "I'm meeting Pete for dinner tonight. Perhaps I might set up another appointment?"

General Wade watched her gather all the pages of figures and replace them in her portfolio. "Bring Pete," he declared, escorting her to the door. "Rebecca will love having young folks to fuss over again. Shall we say eight o'clock?"

Pepper hesitated a moment longer. She cast a quick glance at the rigid back of her adversary, knowing full well she should share the blame for his insubordination. Her stomach tightened. Should she fess up to her part in the little incident, or let the officer meet the general's wrath alone?

"Eight will be fine," she said firmly, hastening through the door.

"DEVLIN SHAUNESSY WADE." The general made a slow circle around Dev's ramrod-stiff form as he drawled each syllable of his son's name. "What's this tommyrot I hear about you and General Huston's wife? Has D.C. run out of single women, or what?"

Dev didn't break his stance. "Sir," he spat out, "perhaps this time your pipeline didn't leak you the truth. But please don't waste any time worrying. I assure you I'm going to clear my name. Then I'm going to resign my commission."

In the deathlike silence that followed his announcement, Dev watched a muscle working in the older man's jaw. At last, the general gave a slight shake of his head and returned to the door, opening it. "Don't be foolish, Devlin. Go on home, son," he said more gently. "And don't worry your mother—she knows none of this. Rebecca's been fussing over this dinner since she found out you were stopping by, and if she finds out you've been on base this long without coming home, we'll both be doing K.P.''

"Am I being dismissed?" Dev asked curtly, remaining at attention. He was not yet ready to forgive, and still spoiling for a confrontation.

"Dismissed!" the general barked, slipping into his role of commander again. "But count on this, you and I will talk later."

Throwing a smart salute, Dev stalked out without a word. It seemed the old man just couldn't leave off giving orders, he thought. And who in blazes was Pete, anyway?

CHAPTER TWO

FRIDAY, FORT BLISS, TEXAS

Rrring.

"Raul, you old so-and-so, it's Wyndom here! I just saw your Mary Kate. Couldn't believe it—she's the spitting image of Maggie. Where have all the years gone? Makes me feel my age, I don't mind telling you.

"What's that? Of course you have my sympathy raising a beautiful daughter on an army post. By the way, Raul, my son Devlin is being assigned to you. He's six-four, handsome as the devil, even if I do say so. A bachelor. Needs a good woman.

"How's that? You want Mary Kate married? I admit, they'd make quite a couple. An ideal match. Tell you what I'll do..."

BLISSFULLY UNAWARE of her father's latest plan to find her a husband, Pepper's main concern was keeping the Ferrari under the twenty-mile-an-hour speed limit as she searched for Pete's quarters. All she needed was to get a speeding ticket on General Wade's post. She'd bet if that major had anything to say about it, they'd slap her in irons for a month. Without half trying, the man had already managed to ruin her day.

Oops! Even after stopping to call for directions, she'd driven right by Pete's place, and right by Pete himself. Pepper slammed on the brakes and backed up. He was pacing the sidewalk and hadn't seen her yet. This didn't look like bachelor officers' quarters to her, though. This street of neat stucco houses looked more like family accommodations. But then, Pete never had been predictable.

"Oooh-whee!" Pepper heard her brother's exclamation almost before she saw the stunned expression on his face. She jumped from the car intending to give him a hug. He was already busy examining the body of the Ferrari.

She shook her head, amused. "Does this mean you approve of my car?"

"Pop said you bought a hotrod. I was looking for some old claptrap on its last legs." Pete gave a long low whistle between his teeth. "What did you do, rob the Arizona Bank?"

"Hotrod?" Pepper bristled, then sighed in resignation. "I'm surprised he didn't tell you that since I spent so much money, it should at least work as bait to trap a man. That's what he told Ruben."

Pete chuckled, pausing in his inch-by-inch examination of the car. He held out his hand, palm up. "Gimme the keys. I'm dying to take this baby for a spin."

"Pete." Pepper's tone showed her exasperation. "I haven't seen you in almost a year. Is my car more important, or what?"

Her brother pretended to ponder the question. Then he ruffled her hair lovingly and gave her a quick squeeze. "Only for you, kid, and only because I have a cake sitting in there looking like a forest fire. I lit twenty-five candles after you called a few seconds ago." He urged her toward the house.

"Here I didn't think you'd even remember my birthday," she chided, looping one arm through his.

Pete turned, giving the Ferrari one last longing look. "Sure you don't want to take a quick spin? I'll go snuff those candles."

"Pedro Stuart Rivera!" Pepper placed her hands on her hips, tapped one foot menacingly and glared at him. Pete's midnight eyes smiled back. He looked like a Rivera through and through. His middle name was the only legacy he bore of his Scottish ancestry.

He opened the door and shrugged contritely. "You know, you look like Mother when you do that. Sound like her, too."

Pepper's eyes misted. Her face paled and her lips trembled noticeably.

"Oh, hey, whatever's wrong, I'm sorry." Pete grasped her hand and tugged her toward a gleaming cake. The candles burned low, some tilting askew. In the dim light of the house the whole top of the cake looked as though it were ablaze. He cleared his throat and tried again. "I wouldn't say anything to ruin your birthday for the world. I keep forgetting you never had a chance to know her."

Pepper dabbed at eyes that had begun to fill with tears. "It's funny," she said. "I was thinking of Mother on the way here." She sighed. "It must be something about turning twenty-five and still living under Papa's thumb. And Grandmother Rivera always makes it sound like the Scottish half of me is to blame for the fact I'm still single. What I want is independence. Not marriage. She and Papa refuse to accept that."

"Margaret McTavish Rivera was one beautiful lady, Pepper. Everyone loved her, except maybe Grandmother. She planned for Pop to marry the daughter of a family friend, but I'm sure you've heard that story. And you can't even blame Grandmother. It's part and parcel of her culture. If we lived in Mexico, Pop wouldn't have had a choice, and you, Pepper, would be married. Pop and Grandmother would simply arrange it. So count yourself lucky that they're only pressuring you."

"How do you know they're pressuring me?" Pepper bent to blow out the candles, before turning to look him square in the face. "And they'd better not arrange anything," she said, watching a single candle flame struggle back to life.

"Believe it or not, it's almost as bad for me. Pop always seems to know some nice young woman to set me up with on every post. Did you make a wish on that inferno?" he asked. "You have my permission to wish for old maidhood, although I'll warn you, it will never happen."

"Why?" She snuffed out the final smoking spire. "Grandmother is so quick to point out that even Mother was pregnant with Ruben when she was barely seventeen. Like, not to be married and pregnant by that age is a disgrace." Pepper sniffed, rubbing her cheek. "She already has me branded an old maid."

Pete's smile was part sympathetic, part wry indulgence. "You will not remain single, sister mine, because in a way, Pop hit the nail square. That set of wheels out there will draw every red-blooded male within a hundred-mile radius on both sides of the border. Men are material creatures, and you will have them groveling at your feet by the score. All after your car, of course."

Pepper chuckled softly. All traces of tears had vanished. "I believe you've inadvertently answered my dilemma, Pete. I'll tell Papa to find a man who doesn't covet my car and I'll marry him on the spot. If, as you say, he can't find one, Papa will give up and let me get a place of my own."

Pete pulled out the candles and cut through the cake with a flourish. He handed Pepper the first piece, then grinned and wiggled his eyebrows. "If you ever tire of being a swinging bachelorette, I could probably be persuaded to take that albatross of a car off your neck. But not the payments." He slapped a fork into her other hand. "Don't eat too much cake. I'm going to take you out on the town to celebrate the big two-five."

She almost choked on the cake and Pete pounded her on the back. "I forgot to tell you." She made a face. "General Wade invited us to a dinner party at his home tonight. I couldn't turn him down because he wants me to bring the cot. Selling him on the prototype is the whole reason I'm here. That and seeing you, of course."

Pete pretended serious contemplation. "I don't know, Pepper. You'd make me dress up and rub elbows with top brass on my day off?" He shrugged lightly. "However, I could be bribed into giving up enchiladas at El Greco's, the best Mexican restaurant in all of Texas, if you let me drive the Ferrari to General Wade's house—the long way."

"Done." She threw up her hands. "Hey, you drive a hard bargain—so to speak. But you're not bad. For an officer."

Pete's eyes narrowed. "Still carrying on your petty vendetta against officers, Sis? I thought you'd have outgrown that by now. Some of the best men I know are officers. Yours truly included."

She set her plate down with a thud and turned away. Pepper had never admitted to anyone in the family why she disliked officers. It *was* petty, and it had happened a long time ago, when she was an emotional, impressionable seventeen. She'd fallen hard for a handsome captain. But she'd soon found out that the captain was only interested in using her infatuation to get to Papa and gain rank. The officer neglected to mention a fiancée he'd left in Ohio. At the time it had been devastating to learn via the grapevine that the man had taken his new promotion and his new bride to his next duty station in Germany. In retrospect, it was only embarrassing.

"Let's not argue on my birthday, Pete. You and Papa think officers were born exalted. I happen to think most of them are pompous and overbearing. Some would sell their own mothers to the highest bidder for a gold bar. Besides, if you really want to test drive the Ferrari, you'll let me think what I like."

"I guess you're entitled," he said grudgingly, "but I have to admit I think you're prejudiced. Suppose you hit the shower first. I presume you won't mind enjoying the luxury of an officer's quarters. I'm house-sitting for Colonel Breckenridge and his wife while they're on temporary duty in Spain. I promise not to tell him you think he's overbearing, and maybe—if you treat me right—I won't give your biases away to General Wade tonight."

Sticking out her tongue at him, Pepper trailed a finger through the thick chocolate frosting on her piece of cake, then slowly licked it off. Unbidden, her thoughts turned to the handsome officer she'd met in General Wade's office. Her heart rate shifted into high gear. It stood to reason that the man was already spoken for, but out of curiosity, maybe tomorrow she'd casually describe him, just to see if Pete could supply a name. Today, the entire encounter loomed much too large in her mind. And right now, she'd better check in with Papa. She'd promised to call when she arrived at Pete's. *Coward, coward.* The taunt goaded inside her head. *You really want to ask who that man is.* Pepper hurried toward the telephone, refusing to listen to her subconscious.

Moments later, she reentered the dining room, a frown marring her brow.

"What's the matter, Sis? Did the old man give you the third degree?"

"No." She shook her head and shrugged. "That's what puzzles me. He didn't. In fact, he said to stay as long as I liked, and didn't even demand I check in before starting back. He just suggested stopping to visit both Mike and Ruben." She plopped into a chair and stared morosely at the remaining cake.

Pete pulled out a chair beside her. "Well, maybe there's hope for ole Pops yet. Why are you looking so glum? What could he possibly be up to three hundred miles away?"

"Did I say I thought he was up to something?" Pepper's gaze became remote. "But he is, isn't he? I just wish I knew what it could be."

"Geez, but you are a suspicious woman." Pete patted Pepper's arm. "Still, you're probably right. If there's anything we all learned early on, it's that when Pop gets too agreeable, watch out, the ax is about to fall." Her brother, too, stared balefully at his second slice of cake.

"Say, before I forget—" he waved a fork in the air "—I promised a friend you'd take his pup back to Sierra Vista. He was transferred and didn't have any place to put the dog. His pickup was loaded down."

"Pete, you didn't." Pepper straightened. Forgetting her father for the moment, she set her half-eaten cake aside. "Just what I need—a smelly dog in my new car."

"I'll give him a bath." Pete made a cross over his heart the way he always had when they were kids. "He'll be good company for you," he wheedled. "It's a long boring trip by yourself."

Pepper chuckled. "You didn't talk this over with Papa, did you? Is that why he was so agreeable?"

"No, I swear!" Pete crossed his heart again.

"Hey, I believe you. I'll take the blasted dog. Provided you check out the air conditioner in my car. It's on the fritz." She took another swipe at the frosting. "What's his name, anyhow? Or is it a her?"

"A him, and his name is Smedley," Pete replied. "Checking your air will be an even trade for transporting him."

"Smedley! What kind of a name is that for a dog? Sounds more like the butler in an Agatha Christie novel."

Pete wolfed down the final chunk of his cake and grinned. As he'd done ever since they were kids, he got his way. And as always, he was adept at changing the subject. "What is the uniform going to be for tonight's shindig? Should I dress to impress?"

"Why would you ask me that? Wear something comfortable." Pepper rose, stretched, then gathered up the dirty plates and headed through the door leading to the kitchen.

"Sis," Pete chided affectionately, "you know what the head shed is like. They usually dress to kill. Or overkill."

Dumping the plates into the sink with a clatter, Pepper whirled to face her brother. "I suppose you plan to use this event to gain another rank or whatever. Show off to the brass. Well, sorry, but I won't be able to help. I didn't bring anything dressy, so the Wades will have to take me as I am."

"Look, Pepper. I'm not bucking for any gold braid. I'm well aware that you'd like to thumb your nose at all things military. If we're as bad as all that, I can't understand why you market your inventions to us. I guess you and I will never see eye to eye, but you should know me well enough to know I don't crease my pants with vinegar, either." He took her arm gently. "Just remember, we're going to this party because *you* were invited—not me. Now go take your shower and get ready."

Her laugh sounded hollow. "It's not the military as such I dislike, but the way it commands your whole life. I can't really explain it, but maybe you'll understand what I mean after you see the only dress I brought. It's not exactly conventional. Then watch how all the military types react tonight."

Pete chuckled and pointed her toward the bath. "Ah, Pepper, I'd probably worry if you suddenly turned conventional. Now go. I'll bring in your bags and check the air. Don't want to ride in a sweatbox if I have to be in my dress duds."

PETE WAS THE SOLE REASON for their late arrival at the Wade party. Pepper complained that they were far later than what could be considered fashionable. Pete's long way around not only used up half her gas, but left them to walk a good distance, because everyone else had arrived on time and taken up all the parking spaces near the house. And that was only part of it; her red heels weren't meant for walking on rough concrete, and from the number of cars already there, Pete had also blown her chance of concluding business with the general early.

"If I'd known you were going to drive by way of Houston," she grumbled, "I would've taken a cab."

Pete tried to pull the plastic tube containing the cot out of her hands, but she shook off his offer with a glare.

"Go ahead, act like a shrew. A deal is a deal. You said I could take the long way." He buttoned his suit jacket and made one last check of his tie in the beveled glass of the carved oak door before ringing the doorbell.

Pepper bit back another comment as the door was opened by a statuesque blonde in an elegantly simple black cocktail dress. She balanced a tray of champagne glasses with one hand, and waved Pete and Pepper in with the other. While the woman was occupied in closing the door, Pete leaned toward Pepper and whispered, "Some maid service the top brass has." He eyed the deep V in the back of the blonde's dress.

Pepper turned, arching one brow disapprovingly. She hissed her brother's name, discreetly kicking him in the shins, before offering the woman pertinent information. "I'm Pepper Rivera, and though I don't always like to admit it—" she paused, giving a long-suffering sigh "—this is my brother Pete. General Wade is expecting us." As she'd hoped, the blonde returned her smile.

"I'm a friend of Mrs. Wade's." The hostess aimed a so-there look in Pete's direction. "You're just in time to toast the prodigal son. Grab a glass of bubbly, scoot on into the library and I'll be seeing you later."

Pete started to take a glass for himself and one for Pepper, then as though suddenly remembering his manners, asked if he could carry the tray. Pepper was left staring after the two, open-mouthed and without a glass of champagne, because the blond beauty had been quick to relinquish her heavy burden and link a hand tipped with brightly polished nails through Pete's arm.

Pepper could have cheerfully bonked him on the head with her plastic cylinder. Yet if this had happened while the Riveras were all living under one roof, she would have taken it in stride. Raul had always insisted the boys look after her, and she was forever being shuffled from one to the other. Especially if one of them ran into a woman he was trying to impress. It just hadn't happened in some time, and never without another brother waiting in the wings to be her escort.

Annoyed with Pete and feeling abandoned, Pepper entered the crowded study alone. Her shock when she saw the guest of honor immediately stilled her anger. Pepper stared at the profile of the handsome major, rising head and shoulders above the crowd, hardly believing her eyes. Her lips formed a surprised *oh*.

Devlin Wade stood, only pretending to relax, on a raised stone hearth. With eyes half-closed, he was suffering through his father's long-winded welcome-home speech. In truth, he was chafing to get on with the talk the general had promised him. He was plotting his next move when his gaze caught the redhead's rocketing entry into the room, and he realized, however reluctantly, that he hadn't given up looking for her. As he studied her, Dev's fingers tightened reflexively, almost snapping the stem of the delicate crystal wineglass he'd been cradling for an eventual toast. Well, what had he expected to see in a woman of her type, after all? *Not this,* he admitted, glowering.

Light from the glittering chandelier set the exotic newcomer's loosely coiffed hair aflame like the glowing halo of a Roman candle. The peasant-styled dress she wore was made of some crushed gauzelike fabric that draped snugly over her breasts in a blaze of red. Ha! Someone must have told her there was power in wearing red.

Deliberately glacial, Dev let his eyes follow the ripple of material as it feathered into orange, then sunshine yellow below a slender waist, past trim hips encased in hot pink to end in handkerchief points of shocking purple that swirled enticingly around her shapely calves. His eyes widened disapprovingly, yet he didn't look away. Gentleman Win's voice droned on and on, but Dev had completely lost what he was saying.

In a room filled with basic black, the woman from the red Ferrari looked like a Gypsy. Without taking his eyes from her outline, Dev suddenly felt his icy indifference change to unbidden heat, which licked like wildfire through his stomach. The fact that he resented feeling anything didn't stop his palms from sweating or his ears from ringing.

Lifting his glass, Dev tossed back the chilled champagne, dropping abruptly back to earth on the wave of laughter washing upward from the crowd. It took him a few moments to realize his father had stopped midsentence and was staring at him curiously.

Damn, he thought. That was the second—no, third—time the woman had caused him to lose his cool. In one day. And he rarely lost it.

General Wade followed the line of his son's gaze, then smiling, made a swift recovery and raised his glass for the toast. "That's what being stationed at the Pentagon will do for you, folks." He winked at Dev as he joked. "Washington is always pressing us to get to the point, so I will. Here's to your continued success, Devlin. The best man for any job has always been a Wade." He clinked his full glass against Dev's empty one. The younger man's scowl darkened as those gathered in the room agreed with a hearty, "Hear, hear!"

Pepper froze in her tracks when she realized that the man being toasted was not a figment of her imagination, but none other than the officer who had claimed so many of her thoughts since she'd left him earlier in General Wade's office. Never once had she imagined him to be the general's son.

She felt a twinge of resentment that had started the moment his smoldering blue gaze had practically undressed her. The twinge was gaining in strength as his obvious dislike at what he saw now left her shivering from cold in the center of a restless throng of strangers. Glancing around nervously, Pepper realized her flamboyance did set her apart from the other guests. She shouldn't have been surprised— wasn't this exactly the reaction she'd expected?

She tilted her head. So the man called Devlin was Gentleman Win's heir-apparent. Well, la-di-da...it didn't give him license to undress her with his eyes. And how like an officer to feel he had the right to do just that.

Feeling the need to cool down her burst of hot temper, Pepper grabbed a glass from a passing waiter and gulped the vintage champagne without savoring its taste. No wonder General Wade had seemed distressed today, she thought, grimacing. Clearly there was nothing of the gentlemanly father visible in the son. Her father's old friend now claimed all of her sympathy.

The crowd was moving again, breaking up into small groups and chatting away like old friends. Pepper cast a glance around the room, looking for Pete. She was still put out by his defection. Her random search revealed only the younger Wade, who was traveling a path destined to cross hers at any moment. Unable to explain why she didn't want to meet him on his home turf, Pepper turned and fled.

The door she chose for her exit led to the kitchen. Pepper hovered in the opening, wondering which way to turn next. A tall woman whose hair glistened in a sleek black chignon was tasting something a plump man wearing a chef's hat and apron offered her from a wicked-looking fork. The older woman stopped tasting as Pepper entered, and lifted one eyebrow questioningly.

"Excuse me." Pepper wet her lips, clutching the cot case in one hand and an empty champagne glass in the other. Placing the glass on a counter, she backed slowly away.

For just an instant, the woman frowned. Then she smiled and held out a hand. "Wait. I know you." The smile faded and a question slid back into the crystal blue eyes. "Don't I?"

Pepper stared hard. The eyes looked familiar, but not the face. She shook her head. "I don't think so," she said. "I'm Mary Kate Rivera. Everyone calls me Pepper. I'm here to discuss the purchase of my cot with General Wade. However, I can see this is not a good time or place for business. I'll call his secretary on Monday and arrange another appointment."

"That's it," exclaimed the woman. "You're Maggie Rivera's daughter. What a likeness." Her smile blossomed full and wide, softening all the sharp angles of her fine-boned face. "That's why you seemed so familiar to me. Maggie and I were about your age when we shared a close friendship. The kind only wives of new officers on lonely outposts can share. Ruben and Manuel were toddlers then, and Maggie was pregnant with her third. I so envied her." A wistful expression filled the beautiful eyes. "Wyndom mentioned you were coming tonight. Seeing you now, I realize I've always envied Maggie's having a daughter, too." Her pale hand fluttered, twisting a double strand of pearls circling a slender throat.

Pepper clutched the case tighter. Color drained from her face. For years she'd pored over pictures of the wildly vi-

vacious Maggie Rivera. It was difficult for her to imagine
this gentle, refined lady as a friend of her mother's. Pepper
opened her mouth to ask more questions, but no words
came.

The door swung in, almost hitting her. Pepper jumped.
Her heart sank another level as she stared into the frosty
eyes of Devlin Wade. But his glance skipped over her, seeking instead the face of the older woman. As Pepper edged
around him toward the door, it struck her that the two
looked very much alike. Of course, she should have known
immediately. The woman was General Wade's wife.

"Devlin." His mother beamed. "So your father finally
ran out of steam. About time, I must say. How that man
does go on." She smiled indulgently. "Now we can serve the
meal." Rebecca Wade beckoned the cook with a slim hand.
Then, easily and companionably, she linked one arm with
her son's and one with Pepper's, moving both of them deftly
through the kitchen door.

"I don't know if you two have had a chance to meet." She
smiled, not slowing their pace. "Devlin, this is the daughter of General Raul Rivera, an old and dear friend of your
father's and mine. Her mother, Maggie, and I were friends
and neighbors before either of you were born. It was a time
when I'd despaired of ever having children." Mrs. Wade
paused just outside the door and patted Dev's arm lovingly. "In fact," she said, turning toward Pepper, "I recall
now, Wyndom mentioned that your father's going to be
Devlin's new commanding officer."

Dev stopped dead. He whirled on Pepper. "You mean to
tell me that your father is the commander at Fort
Huachuca?" His brows drew together, almost meeting over
a sharply defined nose.

"More's the pity for him," Pepper returned with equal
fervor, "especially if he has to deal with your sort." Then
she recoiled in shock at finding herself bordering on rudeness. This officer meant nothing to her—and she wanted to
make it clear that their paths need not cross again. Her only
interest in being here tonight, and her only interest in the

Wade family, was selling her cot to the general. Then she could get a place of her own and start her new independent life. She had to succeed in convincing Gentleman Win. She *would* succeed. If her heart didn't thunder out of her chest first.

Rebecca Wade's expression showed distress as she gazed from her son to the daughter of her old friend. It changed to one of relief when her husband whisked up.

"Ah, Mary Kate," General Wade announced in a jovial voice. "So glad you finally arrived. I see my wife and son have introduced themselves." He rubbed both hands together briskly. "Well, well. Having you all together will make my announcement easier." A twinkle of self-satisfaction lit his gaze, touching each of them in turn.

Dev and Pepper were still wearing expressions of doom, and Rebecca appeared a bit confused. Wyndom Wade reached out to pull the plastic cylinder from Pepper's stiff fingers. "Do you have another one of these with you, Mary Kate?"

She nodded, without pausing to give it thought.

"Good, good." The general waved the tube under Devlin's nose. "I'm very interested in this young lady's invention, Dev. However, my committee has neither the time nor the resources to test it properly. Since both of you are heading for Fort Huachuca soon, I have hit upon a most expedient solution. The two of you can test the cot while camping out through New Mexico and Arizona. As the terrain at each campsite will be different, this offers the perfect trial." He grinned broadly, ignoring the shocked response of his audience.

"Impossible," snapped Dev, thrusting out a hand in denial at the same moment Pepper shook her head and stoutly said, "No."

The general's head swiveled, taking in first one and then the other of his young companions. "That's an order, Dev," he said softly, pressing the cot into his son's outstretched palm.

Pepper's mouth opened in protest, then closed. She could see the whole project being scrapped. If General Wade didn't approve her cot, she could see her independence flying out the window. She could also see her father's continuing parade of eligible bachelors. Pepper bit her tongue.

Pete came up behind her then, sliding one arm around her waist. He bent down to kiss her warmly on the cheek. "Why so serious, kid? Eat, drink and be merry. After all, you've reached the quarter-century mark today and that's something to celebrate."

"Why, Mary Kate!" the general exclaimed. "You should have told me it was your birthday. We would have had a cake." Even as Gentleman Win smiled and spoke, he studied the intruder. Devlin, too, had transferred his venomous glare to the handsome new arrival in their midst.

"Pete." Pepper welcomed her brother with a smile, happy that she no longer faced the Wades alone. "You've met General Wade, I assume?" At Pete's nod, she nestled her head in the hollow of his shoulder and moved closer under his protective arm. Reluctantly she admitted that at times like this, it was nice to have family to lean on.

"Of course I know Pete." Quickly recovering his aplomb, the general reached for Pete's hand and pumped it heartily. "I just didn't recognize you out of uniform, Captain." His smile broadened as he took in his son's unyielding stance. Not introducing the two, the wily general sidestepped Dev, casually moving Rebecca, along with Pepper and Pete, toward the dining room. "Come," he invited, "there are other people here I'd like you to meet."

Thoroughly irritated, Devlin watched his father lead the group away. Well, they'd just see about those orders when he and Gentleman Win finished their promised talk, he thought, adding nastily under his breath, "Civilians don't take orders."

And in the fleetest of moments before the cozy foursome disappeared from his sight, Devlin let himself indulge in a tiny bit of West Point pride he normally would have scoffed at—downright, gut-level pleasure in knowing that, at least for the moment, he outranked Pete.

CHAPTER THREE

MONDAY, FORT BLISS, TEXAS

Rrring.

"Hello Miguel? Pete here. Pop asked me to call and let you know when Pepper's heading out. Today is the day. She's planning to spend the night at Caballo Lake. Hey—you got a notion what Pop's up to this time?

"No? Well, call me if you find out. So long."

Click.

THREE DAYS was not nearly enough time to prepare for purgatory, which was how Pepper viewed her upcoming trek with Major Wade. Moreover, she couldn't believe her father had given his sanction. Certain that he'd never agree to her traveling with a man, she'd phoned to tell him the news. Instead of exploding as Pepper had anticipated, he'd praised the Wade family and given this venture his blessing.

The remainder of her vacation with Pete hadn't gone well, either, not after the general dropped his little bombshell at the party. Once Papa had given his approval, Pete found the situation entirely too humorous to suit Pepper. Only today, after she'd threatened not to deliver Smedley, had her brother finally stopped teasing. Now Benedict Arnold was off collecting and bathing the animal—and washing the Ferrari, she hoped—while she packed for the trip.

"I ask you," she muttered aloud for the umpteenth time, "what kind of brother would send his only sister alone into the wilderness with the likes of Devlin Wade?"

"A rat," she answered, fastening the last quiet snap on the pack—her own invention. "The way these military men stick together is criminal."

Pepper hoisted the pack and adjusted the straps. "It would serve him right if I refused to take that dumb dog. If I know Pete, a bath will mean running Smedley through the car wash with the Ferrari." Still muttering, Pepper marched toward the door.

"I can't wait to see this pup. Probably some neurotic, bedraggled poodle, afraid of his own shadow. A week in the wilds with Smedley and Major Boston Baked Bean should have me begging to live forever with Papa."

Over the course of the weekend, Pepper's research on the life and times of Devlin Wade had turned up the information that he was born in Boston at his mother's family estate—an estate of considerable wealth. Among other things, those tidbits had become significant enough to hold against him.

Getting stuck with a helpless city slicker was the crowning blow, she grumbled, slamming the door behind her. Then her grumbling ceased. Before her at the curb stood the clean but still dripping Ferrari. Pete had one arm looped over the open car door, his heels digging furrows in the sand. Tightly clutched in his other hand was a short tether attached to at least fifty pounds of bouncing, wiggling, loudly woofing Old English sheepdog.

Dismayed, Pepper watched as one removed, until a dark sedan pulled in behind the Ferrari and out stepped Devlin Wade, combat ready. Pepper snickered. She couldn't believe that in this heat, even a city man would wear full military garb—but there he was, living proof. Her snicker turned into an outright laugh as she watched the friendly dog land muddy paws on the major's freshly polished black boots.

Though Pete dug in harder, the muddy paws walked up Wade's carefully bloused fatigues, landing squarely in the middle of his neatly creased khaki shirt. And if that wasn't indignity enough, the dog's tongue began vigorously licking Major Wade's set and angry face.

Pepper noticed Gentleman Win leaning out the back door of the sedan and did her best to smother her smile. However, the general only gave her a brief wave before tossing his son's gear onto the ground. Aiming a quick salute Devlin's way, he slammed the car door and motioned his driver on. Pepper was much too interested in the scene before her to wonder about the general's hasty retreat.

All at once her amused gaze met and locked with Devlin Wade's furious glare. Today his crystal-blue eyes were storm-dark and turbulent as an angry sea. It was as though fiery fingers tightened in Pepper's stomach and sent ripples of heat skittering along her tense muscles. Eyes like Major Wade's didn't belong on someone dressed for combat, unless the war was in the bedroom. Pepper shivered, yet refused to look away.

"Control this animal." Dev held her gaze. His clipped tone clearly stated that he expected to be obeyed.

Pete looked aghast and did his best to snap off a salute to his superior. "Geez, I'm sorry, Major." He pulled back harder on the leash. Sweat popped out on his brow as he took in Dev's muddy shirt.

"Sit." This time Dev's voice was murderous. Still his eyes held Pepper's, and for an instant, she almost followed his command herself.

To his credit, Smedley backed away and sat. He still wiggled all over and thumped his poor excuse for a tail on the ground, but he didn't leap at the major.

Because Smedley's eyes were completely hidden in a mop of gray fur, Pepper failed to see that both dog and major had turned their attention on her as she left the safety of the porch. She was quite ready to tell Pete that she wouldn't take Smedley three feet, let alone three hundred miles, when Major Wade voiced another command.

"That beast is unruly. Put him in a kennel." Carelessly he flipped out sunglasses and settled them disdainfully on his nose. Then he began swiping at the dirt on his shirt, but because it was wet, he only made it worse.

Pepper flew to Smedley's defense. She didn't like the light-headed attraction she felt for this man, the way looking at him made her knees wobble like newly set Jell-O. She needed to put him in his place. Needed to establish turf. Her turf.

"He's just a pup," she admonished. "He is neither unruly nor a beast."

Overzealous, the pup landed on his defender. All fifty pounds of him behind two massive paws hit Pepper squarely on the shoulders. Down she went, backpack, dufflebag and all, struggling under a mountain of fur. A wet tongue bathed her cheek, tickled her ear and tangled in her loosened curls. She thought she recognized Pete's voice swearing, and thought she heard the major's deep laughter, but first and foremost, her struggle was sheer self-preservation.

Dev's sudden burst of laughter was short-lived. The sight of Pepper's long length of creamy leg, curving enticingly from vibrant orange satin shorts, stilled his laughter. He swallowed hard, ripped off his sunglasses and passed a none-too-steady hand over his eyes. Dev reminded himself that a man of thirty-two was long past the phase of lusting after a shapely body. Especially not this man—and more specifically, not that body. She was General Rivera's daughter. It would be a cold day in Texas before he looked kindly at a general's relative again—or at any other woman, for that matter.

Pete succeeded in pulling the dog off his sister, but for a brief moment, Pepper still lay sprawled on the ground. Dazed, she moved slowly, trying to right a yellow T-shirt that now showed the effects of Smedley's muddy paws.

Dev did an abrupt about-face, placing hands on hips, legs spread wide. *At least she isn't wearing red today. Though that's a small thing considering the brazenness of the frivolous car she drives. Not to mention those shorts...* Taking an extra second, Devlin resettled his glasses and suddenly realized that his father's car no longer waited at the curb. He rubbed his temple and tried to think clearly. Something about this whole deal had a phony ring. Gentleman Win had been too quick to cut new orders. Testing equipment was not now, nor had it ever been, part of his job. And it wasn't as if he hadn't tried every angle he knew to get out of this farce. His father had a pat answer for everything. Eventually, Dev had given in because he had no intention of resigning until he'd cleared that one black mark from an otherwise spotless record. It was more than a matter of pride. He was a good cryptologist. So, where along the way had he lost his enthusiasm for a puzzle? Usually he enjoyed uncovering the pieces until even the most illogical information became part of a whole. But he seemed to be missing the cornerstone of this puzzle. He only knew that there was some connection with General Rivera's daughter.

Devlin swung back around in time to watch the captain helping his sister unsteadily to her feet. A smile touched his lips. What an interesting jigsaw shape Mary Kate Rivera made. He eyed the license plate on her car—RED HOT. Pepper, his father had said her nickname was. Yes, he'd agree. Devlin sniffed, hardening his resolve. She was too hot for him to handle, if he intended to keep his interim record clean enough to resign anytime soon. A week on the road with General Rivera's daughter promised to be about seven days too many.

Dev's lips dropped to narrow slits as he studied Pepper, now deep in conversation with her brother. His father had been expounding a lot on the joys of marriage over the weekend. Could it be that General Rivera's daughter needed a husband? He frowned. No—marriages weren't arranged anymore. The very thought was uncivilized. He looked pensively around him at the sun-scorched landscape. But then, this land was uncivilized, and if the reports he'd dug up on General Rivera could be believed, he was a man who lived by the old codes.

Dev continued to mull it over. He would go along with testing the cot because he was headed in her direction, anyway. But otherwise, he was through being outflanked by his father. And he, for one, didn't need help choosing a wife—not that he was looking for a wife.

"So where's our Jeep?" he asked, hefting his duffle and breaking into their conversation with a throaty growl.

Pete had a viselike grip on Smedley's collar. He was almost on his haunches behind the large woolly dog. "No Jeep, Major," he gasped. One hand left the animal to make a sweeping gesture, indicating the Ferrari. "You'll be traveling in high style this trip."

Pepper's pulse leaped as Dev's dark brows arched above his mirrored lenses. She watched his angular jaw tighten.

"We're going on maneuvers in that?" His distaste for the Ferrari dripped from every cultured syllable.

"Not maneuvers, Major Wade," Pepper taunted sweetly, stepping close. "Camping. We are going camping. In case it has slipped your mind, I'm a civilian. You're the one who was ordered to make this trip. I'm simply going home."

Dev had the sudden feeling that nothing about this woman was simple. He shrugged. "Maneuvers, camping, whatever. Do you expect us to travel rough terrain in that flashy, flimsy, overpriced bucket of bolts?"

Pete stood up, edging close to his sister. Smedley sensed freedom and lunged for Dev again, woofing wildly. Ignoring the melee, Pete hissed low in Pepper's ear. "I don't believe this. A man who thinks a Ferrari is a bucket of bolts. This man definitely isn't falling all over your car, Sis. By George, I think we've found the perfect candidate for Pop. Perhaps I'll call him tonight."

Pepper's gaze left Dev's broad shoulders, again splayed by Smedley's furry paws, to focus on Pete's mischievous grin. For the space of a few rapid heartbeats her imagination ran wild, giving her a quick sketch of what marriage to Devlin Wade might entail. It was an image vivid enough to cause her a moment of sheer panic. "You wouldn't dare," she whispered fiercely, backing away from her brother's triumphant wink.

Nearby a car horn honked loudly. All three of them turned to look. "There's my ride. Gotta go, Sis." Pete transferred the loop of Smedley's leash to Pepper's wrist. He gave her a quick peck on the cheek and dashed a precision salute toward Dev. "Have a great trip, you two. No doubt about it, Sis, he's the one." Pete whistled a few bars of an almost unrecognizable tune.

Off-key though he was, Pepper thought she picked up a faint resemblance to the wedding march. "Not funny, Pete," she shouted ineffectually after his retreating form. Arms folded, she watched him climb into the waiting car, which left with a great squealing of tires. "For your information, Pete Rivera, if I ever do get married, I'll never marry a military man—much less an officer," she muttered under her breath, all the while ignoring the icy foreboding that swept through her veins.

Sensing Devlin's stare, she turned mechanically to face him, pasting a bright smile on her lips.

"Maybe you'd like to tell me what all that nonsense was about?" His tone was low, his jaw rigid.

"Nothing. Nothing that concerns you, Major," she answered stiffly. "My brothers, one and all, share a sick sense of humor. It's an old family joke that's worn very thin. Now, I suggest we load up and get moving. I'd like to set up camp in daylight."

Dev knew something had happened and he'd been left out of the circle. Pete Rivera had seemed a nice-enough fellow. They'd talked that night after dinner, once Dev had learned the captain was Mary Kate's brother. Still, he had no reason to trust any of them. Maybe he should find himself another way of getting to the base in Sierra Vista. If he had any sense at all, he would.

"Where's this dog going?" Devlin shifted his bag to the other hand. "And I use the term *dog* loosely."

"With us." Opening the car door, Pepper whipped out an old rag and began drying Smedley's muddy feet. "The dog is headed for his owner in Sierra Vista. Right on our way."

"Two adults and a mutt crammed in a sardine can? No way," Dev declared hotly. "Anyway, dogs don't take to me."

Pepper stopped wiping and led Smedley to the open car door. "I can understand that." Holding back the seat, she smirked broadly as he jumped right in as though he'd been riding in the cramped space of the Ferrari every day of his life. "Well, perhaps you'd like to call your father and tell him you've changed your mind. Smedley was invited first." Pepper dusted off her hands. *So it's not quite the truth—what the heck.* With minimal effort she loaded her gear into the small car.

Before she could blink, Dev had tossed his pack and duffle in on top of hers. "I just bet you'd like me to do that. Well, you'd better get used to having a shadow, lady, because I intend to figure out what little scheme you, your brother and my father are hatching by the time we reach Fort Huachuca."

Pepper stared, confusion written on her face, as he slid easily into the driver's seat. "Wait just a darn minute," she said, blustering. "I'm not one of your subordinates. See," she shouted, yanking the sleeve of her T-shirt under his nose. "No stripes. And don't you forget it. Furthermore, this is *my* flimsy bucket of bolts, as you were so quick to call it. I'll drive."

Dev's gaze rested at eye level with her ripe contours. He lifted his dark glasses, then fearful of exposing the sudden yearning he could feel smoldering behind his eyes, he looked away. He didn't want to want her. There was already one trumped-up scandal to wipe off his slate. Unconsciously his fingers curled around the wheel. General Rivera's daughter would tempt a saint, and because he'd never pretended to be a saint, he suspected she would test him in every way known to man. His father couldn't have issued a harsher penance, Dev thought ruefully—if he was, indeed, expected to use this trip to repent.

Without saying a word, he slid from the car, walked around and folded his long limbs into the passenger seat. A cold mask slid into place. This tangy hot tamale wasn't his type, he told himself again. She was far too headstrong and much too independent for his taste.

Pepper arched one brow questioningly. The look he'd given her had shaken her composure. Strange man, Major Devlin Wade. Strange because he set her heart pounding. Strange because, until now, she thought she had sound reason for disliking officers, and this one went about sneaking through her defenses, scaling old barriers. She'd have to be on constant alert. She couldn't afford to trust him. After all, Pete had been able to find out very little background information on the Pentagon's prize cryptologist. Mostly he'd learned about the major's reputation for squiring only the most poised and beautiful women to official events. But this was not an official event, and the major had made it quite clear that he was here only because he'd been ordered. All of which suited her just fine. Pepper scooted into the driver's seat. In a life already filled with overbearing males, she didn't need another. And since the opinionated major hadn't argued about her right to drive, she must have won this preliminary round in their ongoing tussle of wills. Calmly she fastened her seat belt, determined to bluff her way through whatever came next.

"Sit," she snapped at Smedley, who'd draped his big head over her right shoulder and snuffled contentedly. Wade had allowed himself only the barest flicker of response to her challenge. Without looking directly at him, she knew when he replaced his dark glasses and slid down in the seat, his head against the headrest. Pepper just wished she could be sure he'd closed his eyes. She wasn't firm enough in her convictions to drive some three hundred miles with Washington's boy wonder watching her from beneath hooded lids. Dev Wade was a wonder all right, she admitted, but he was every inch a man.

After a few miles, the dog slept. The air conditioner made a funny noise and kicked off, but the major didn't budge. In spite of the heat that began to build, Pepper could feel the tension ebb as the miles slipped by. She enjoyed driving. And Wade was easy to look at, surprisingly gentle in sleep. She found herself wanting to know more about him. Wanting to know everything about him.

Papa was always dragging home eligible military men, and she'd never wanted to know more about any of them. She grimaced. Well, not since that painful time when she'd been seventeen and had so unwisely offered her young, naive heart.

She glanced at Major Devlin Wade, a general's son. This man wouldn't need to impress her father. Still, that long-ago captain had been a West Pointer, too....

Throughout Pepper's studied scrutiny, Dev pretended to sleep, although he couldn't have dropped off to save himself. One-hundred-degree heat blistered through his side window. Any breeze that wafted in wafted right back out the sunroof. Trickles of sweat flowed freely down his chest. He was reluctant to admit that some of the heat was generated by his proximity to Pepper's bare leg and the inviting satin of her hot-orange shorts. His fingers itched to touch her skin just to see if it was as soft as it looked, but he controlled the urge. He told himself he wanted city-chic. He told himself he wanted cool. But he realized he wasn't adept at lying.

Devlin was afraid she'd catch him peeking through half-closed lids. It would interrupt this ridiculous fantasy he was weaving and lure him into conversation. He needed time to study the situation, time to figure her out and work through this ambivalence he was feeling.

Pepper thought she saw the major's eyelids flicker. Out of the corner of one eye, she noted a fine sheen of sweat beading his brow. Foolish Easterner. He was wearing far too many clothes. Still and all, her heart pounded furiously at the thought of viewing those muscular legs in shorts. Her own T-shirt clung damply. How much was due to the heat and how much to thinking about Major Wade's sculpted muscles framed by a close-fitting tank top? Pepper shook her head, attempting to dispel the vision.

Suddenly the road forked. Las Cruces traffic branched off to the right. Leaning back in the contoured seat, Pepper put pressure on the gas pedal and listened to the hum of the Ferrari's tires on the hot asphalt. She swallowed hard, vowing not to look his way again. Instead she admired how beautifully sky and desert merged on the distant horizon.

As the flash of scenery became no more than a blur, Dev's right hand automatically checked his seat-belt clasp. Pepper caught him in the act. No use pretending he was asleep now. He yawned, giving a deliberately casual stretch.

"Going to a fire, Ms Rivera? Or is the fire us? Where's our air?" He found hiding behind sarcasm easier than watching her, coppery hair leaping and dancing through the sunroof opening. Easier than smelling the scent she wore, which was driving him to distraction. He'd been trying to analyze the potent, exotic fragrance for the past thirty miles. The spicy combination of cinnamon and orange blossom suited her somehow. He tensed as Pepper spoke.

"The Ferrari's air conditioner is acting up. Pete tried to fix it, but he's not the mechanical one in the family. At Burro Peak, I'll have Miguel take a look." She grinned, extending the olive branch. Quick to lose her temper, she was also quick to make up. "And I'm always in a hurry. My brothers are constantly reminding me to slow down. But I suppose Pete revealed all my unsavory vices that night at your party?"

As Dev straightened in the seat, Smedley raised his head, barked and then stretched, too. His ears whipped out through the sunroof along with Pepper's unfurled tresses. Dev turned halfway to get a better look at Smedley and smothered a laugh. Despite the oppressive heat, he felt curiously lighthearted, something he hadn't felt in a long while. He shook his head, then reached out to catch a blowing strand of Pepper's hair and curl it around his own finger. Shaking it loose again, he reminded himself that she was off-limits. Definitely off-limits.

"Your deep dark secrets are still safe," he muttered. "Pete hardly had time to unveil any mysteries after the general railroaded us. And today he was too busy trying to corral this...dog. Do you have some? Deep dark mysteries, that is?" Dev tried to look guileless and still pay close attention to her face as she answered.

Her throaty laugh raised the fine hairs along his arm. "Smedley. Can you believe this mutt's name is Smedley? I had him pictured as a poodle. No one was more surprised than me when I walked out and saw this monster."

She was changing the subject and that made Dev wonder. Surely she was privy to his father's little scheme. In on it, no doubt. At least that was where he'd put his money if he were a betting man. Besides, he hadn't imagined Pete's whispered remarks earlier. Captain Rivera had made it plain enough that they needed a candidate for something... marriage, was it? Dev grasped another lock of Pepper's hair then, as a calculated measure. He let it blow free, watching as the wind whipped it out of reach.

Maybe Wyndom Wade had decided his son needed a wife to cool the scandal back at the Pentagon, he speculated. Who better to serve that purpose than his old friend's daughter? A chill dried the sweat on Devlin's brow. Why would anyone who looked like this stunning redhead need an arranged marriage? When he had that answer, Dev decided, the puzzle would be solved, and by then, with any luck, he'd have figured out how to clear his name.

The hypnotic terrain and his meanderings were making Devlin sleepy again. "Where are we headed?" he asked around a yawn, not completely certain he wanted to hear her answer. "I'm out of my element."

"We've left Texas and we're a few miles into New Mexico now. If we weren't testing the cot, we could make it to Fort Huachuca by tonight. I'm taking the long way, since we have time to kill. I thought you might enjoy camping at Caballo Lake. It's still considered desert but offers a little more greenery. Tenderfeet need breaking in easy. By the way, do you fish?"

"Fishing isn't high on my list of priorities." Dev turned, watching the dog snooze. It wasn't that he couldn't fish. He simply didn't care to. "I prefer to get my fish at a four-star restaurant. I hope you don't expect me to catch my dinner."

Pepper frowned. "We didn't discuss any rules for this outing. I believe in separate, but equal. With five brothers, I too often ended up as chief cook and bottle washer. I learned early that it was every man for himself—or in my case, woman. You do camp?"

"Some," he said, shifting in the seat. "I *am* in the army. Training at West Point isn't like accommodations at the Hilton, you know."

"Yes, but there's camping, and then there's camping. If you get my drift."

Dev twisted in the car's narrow confines and threw one arm over the back of her seat. He wasn't in this desolate country by choice, and he didn't like her reminding him that she was better equipped to handle this adventure than he. Dev thought of the women with whom he'd spent his free time in Washington. Together, they might have enjoyed a day at a museum; he envisioned stateliness. Or they could have chosen to attend the theater; he envisioned tranquility. Devlin stared out the window. What he saw here was a three-star general's bohemian daughter guiding a fast car with a capable hand, through savage countryside. He tensed, feeling an uncommon need to justify his viewpoint before they traveled farther.

Dropping his hand to Smedley's head, Dev faced Pepper and demanded, "What the hell does that last remark of yours mean? Why are you talking in riddles? Camping is sleeping out under the stars and cooking in half-washed utensils. It's checking off the days until you can get home to a decent shower. That is my definition, not Webster's. Now let me remind you, Ms Rivera, I am here only to render an unbiased opinion on the durability of your cot. Period. I wasn't ordered to have fun."

Pepper came up behind a pickup truck sporting off-road tires and passed it as though the four-wheeler were standing still. She turned a frosty gaze his way, keeping her right foot firmly on the gas. "I thought riddles were your specialty, Major, but please, let me be succinct." Her voice fell an octave. "I like to camp. I like to hike. I like to fish. What I don't like is dragging you along." Pepper waved a finger under Dev's nose. "You have a cot, Major. I have a cot. You have gear. I have gear. We share the same transportation, but that's all. I fully intend to enjoy some outdoor sports and pay visits to my brothers along the way. You, Major Wade, may spend your entire time in camp, testing the durability of my cot, if you so desire. Does that meet with your Majorship's approval?"

"Will you just slow this car down?" Dev ignored her scathing tone and, gripping the dash with one hand, continued to glare at her. "I may not enjoy outdoor life, but I enjoy life!"

"I'll just bet you do," she murmured sweetly. "And I'll also bet you especially enjoy indoor sports. If you could test the cot in a carpeted room, equipped with a blonde measuring 36-24-36, you'd probably like it just fine." Pepper tossed out the words, not realizing she'd touched a nerve.

Devlin let his eyelids drop to hide his fury. It was a fury stemming from the unfairness of the situation that had landed him here—the situation, and his father for sending him on this stupid mission. He knew that. But he didn't like to hear Pepper Rivera, a woman he found himself attracted to against his will, throwing it back in his face.

"You're pretty free with your accusations, Ms Rivera. Do you think having a general for a father entitles you to privileged information about classified orders and gives you license for bad manners?"

Dumbfounded, Pepper took a moment to stare at him. She didn't have the vaguest idea what he was talking about. Nor did she know why he suddenly had murder written in his eyes. She was beginning to suspect, however, that she was missing some pretty crucial facts about Major Devlin Wade and his recent transfer to Fort Huachuca. What else could account for the cold glitter in his eyes? She pulled her gaze from him long enough to swing the wheel sharply to the right. The road she chose was a simple, two-way track, a thin ribbon of concrete curling across a shimmering expanse of sand. The Ferrari swayed from side to side. Smedley hid his head under his paws and began to howl.

Pepper smoothed the furrow between her brows with two fingers. Major Wade sounded as though he thought she owed him an apology, but without more of an explanation, he could think again. She pressed her foot harder on the gas until the Ferrari wound out in a whine.

"This isn't the Daytona 500," Devlin said gruffly near her ear. "Whatever you're trying to prove can wait until we both have our feet on the ground. Even the mutt is scared half to death."

"Oh, that's rich," Pepper sputtered, feeling somewhat defensive despite herself. "Pretend to care about the dog. You're the one who said you didn't like animals. I suppose they teach you at the Point how to keep changing the subject just to weasel your way out of an honest confrontation."

Dev lifted one brow. "I simply said dogs don't take to me." His tone implied more. So, he thought, the Red Hot Pepper didn't like being put on the defensive? She hedged every answer, and she didn't like officers. Once again, Dev found himself wondering what her game was. She didn't seem to want him—or anyone else, either—for a husband. She damn sure wasn't trying to charm him. If anything, she was doing her best to discourage him. But did she honestly not know the effect of bright orange shorts and a skimpy yellow T-shirt? They were hardly discouraging. Whatever she and Gentleman Win were peddling, Dev swore then and there he wasn't buying. If his father wanted the damn cot, he should be the one in God's forgotten acre sleeping on it. And if, as he suspected, Gentleman Win was planning a wedding, the Old Man had better save his money.

As Devlin opened his mouth, ready to lay down his cards with all the facts he thought he had assembled, the Ferrari jerked to a stop amid a cloud of dust, and Pepper announced brightly, "We're here."

All of the revelations he'd planned to spell out vanished through the sunroof, mingling with the blowing sand. His gaze was drawn to a lone, scraggly tree that remotely resembled a pine. But the thing that almost choked him, and really served to still his tongue, was the mad bustle of campers ringing the sand-swept lake. Like a colony of bees, they were all setting up varying degrees of housekeeping on sites as barren and primitive as the one he faced.

"Yuck!" he muttered with distaste under his breath. He put his head in his hands and groaned. Truly, he didn't like anything about camping. Raising his head long enough to look into the eager face of the woman seated next to him and to see the childlike excitement shining from her eyes, Devlin was almost sorry he didn't. Without giving his actions any conscious thought, he reached out one finger and traced the curve of her cheek.

Surprised, Pepper turned, her wistful smile asking for nothing more than his acceptance. Arguments of any type made her uneasy. She had always been first in her family to seek a truce, and she extended the ceasefire now to include her forced companion.

Drawn by her silent plea, Dev leaned toward her parted lips. Slowly his head tilted a fraction, and he might have kissed her then—and he sensed that she might have let him. But Smedley thrust his head between them and barked. So instead of kissing her, Dev pulled back in his seat, announcing brusquely, "You'd better take the mutt outside. Take first choice of real estate, too. Pick your place to test that cot, Ms Rivera. Then I'll pick mine—as far away from the two of you as possible."

CHAPTER FOUR

HAPPY TO HAVE ESCAPED the stifling confines of the car, Pepper ran with Smedley along the edge of the shimmering lake, where the air was a degree or two cooler. Dev's light touch on her cheek had set fires along nerve endings she hadn't known existed. His move toward her was unexpected, and so was the way she felt about it, the way she felt about him. She'd been trying to sort out those feelings, so it had taken longer than normal to set up her tent and assemble her cot.

Pepper paused for a moment's reflection as Smedley stopped to sniff a clump of dry grass. Unwillingly her gaze was drawn to the man she'd left behind.

Devlin Wade was leaning negligently against the bright car, an elbow braced against one door and his chin tucked into the hollow of his fist, and seemed to be studying the terrain.

He'd removed his shirt. Pepper could see it draped across the hood. Far from being the pasty-skinned indoorsman she'd pegged him, Dev's well-muscled torso was positively tanned. Biceps outlined in the late afternoon sun showed a strength only hinted at when they were hidden beneath his tailored shirt.

Smedley snuffled at Pepper's hand, beckoning her to follow. She waved him off, unable to take her eyes from Devlin. Without uniform and medals, the major looked like any other man. No, she admitted reluctantly, not just any man.

No other man had ever made her feel this way. Had ever made her feel . . . like touching his broad chest, dusted ever so nicely with crisp dark hair.

Pepper whirled around, horrified at the path her fantasies were taking. Devlin Wade was a military man, an officer—with or without his government-issue trappings. Officers couldn't be trusted. Pepper had to repeat that fact to recall its significance. Chant the words a few times to remember them.

Smedley shot away, bounding toward the car and the man. Frantically Pepper called him. He stopped, circled, then came panting back. It was a small act, but one that restored her confidence and left her feeling in control. Quickly and before she could look Dev's way again, Pepper chased the dog toward a dock stretching on time-worn wooden piers, fifty feet or so out over the shallow lake.

DEVLIN HADN'T BEEN AWARE of Pepper's assessment, because he was much too preoccupied in trying to determine what had made him think of kissing her in the car. She wasn't his type. He'd long since decided that. Her taste in cars and clothes was outrageous, not at all in keeping with his more conservative tenor. She was military born and bred, and he couldn't wait to get out. Her father was a general . . . and Dev refused to trust her.

Idly he brushed a forefinger over his dry lips. Despite his careful reasoning, the sight of her just now, lit by fiery red-orange splinters from a sinking sun, triggered sudden longings deep inside him. Longings, he told himself, that must be ignored. When he'd finally agreed to this insane request of his father's, he hadn't counted on the lady creating an inferno hot enough to warp old standards and intense enough to forge new ones. Granted, he'd be a fool to deny the attraction, but after Candy Huston's betrayal, he'd be a bigger fool to give in to it. Dev cursed the heat and the Red Hot Pepper under his breath.

He watched her move farther along the lake, out of his sight. *You should have kissed her and been done with it,* a little voice nagged. One simple kiss—hardly a marriage proposal. A kiss, nevertheless, that would allow him command of his life again. *And by the devil, I'll do it, Gentleman Win's subterfuge be hanged.*

One kiss from Mary Kate Rivera, and then he'd put her out of his life—the woman *and* her idea of a camping trip. He looked at the tent she'd singlehandedly erected and thought there was nothing wrong with wanting his women to be sophisticated or worldly. The decision having brought him grim satisfaction, he turned to the Ferrari and began yanking out his gear.

Women seeking sensible careers, if they wanted careers, was one matter. Inventors, quite another. Pepper didn't even look like an inventor, he rationalized, pulling out the tube containing his cot. Inventors were serious men. Bald. Wearing wire-rimmed glasses. Weren't they?

Immersed as Dev was in private contemplation, he hadn't paid attention to the oversize motor home pulling into an adjacent campsite until its resulting dust enveloped him. He laughed, then choked, noting the air-conditioning unit and television antenna gracing the top of the elaborate conveyance. Now *that* was his idea of camping.

Dev couldn't help wondering what Pepper would have to say about its opulence compared to her one-woman tent. She seemed to think only Easterners, like himself, enjoyed creature comforts, but the motor home was sporting Texas plates. Dev dropped his cot and camp equipment in a hollowed-out cleft between where Pepper had staked her claim and where the new arrivals were parked. He didn't do it with any conscious thought of shielding her, but didn't pause, either, to study his motives.

When two women, nearer his age than Pepper's, stepped from the motor home and walked toward him, Dev's thoughts still lingered on Pepper.

"Well, well, Sylvia. Didn't I tell you this campground looked interesting?" The taller of the two women confronted Dev as he returned to the Ferrari for his dufflebag. Startled by the warm familiarity in her voice, he glanced up, meeting her eyes. His were open and wary, hers interested and calculating.

"Hello." Dev's greeting was low-key and reserved. He examined, with some skepticism, the two model-thin women dressed in designer sportswear. Yesterday he might have found them attractive; today he was surprised to feel indifference.

"I'm Patti, spelled with an 'i,'" stated the sleek blonde. "This is Sylvia." She waved crimson-tipped fingernails in the direction of her dark-haired companion. "We just love your wheels." She tittered. "They're exactly what your license plate implies—Red Hot. How about giving us a little spin in your mean machine, Tall, Dark and Handsome?"

Adept at fielding all manner of cocktail-party come-ons, Dev found her little byplay amusing but predictable. He gave a throaty laugh and merely continued rummaging in the car.

The taller woman sidled closer. "We'll offer you a cold beer and stimulating conversation first," she promised. "You're the first man we've seen in two weeks who hasn't been dragging around the little woman and five kids, or been bald and sixty."

This time Dev's laugh was full-bodied and genuine. Out of the corner of one eye he'd observed Pepper's and Smedley's return. And Pepper was making no secret of eavesdropping on their conversation. She made no bones about her contempt, either. Dev wondered whether she would lose that Arctic chill from her eyes if she knew what he really found so amusing about Patti-with-an-"i"—the way Patti had immediately jumped to the conclusion that the Ferrari belonged to him.

"I assure you this car won't hold a wife and five kids," he joked with Patti, leaning easily against the Ferrari's hood and crossing his feet at the ankles. "Barely holds my business associate and her canine companion." Devlin inclined his head in Pepper's direction.

By this time, Patti had made her move and was boldly running a red-tipped fingernail across Dev's bare chest. She looked up to assess the redhead, then gave his chest one last tap with a painted nail before shrugging and backing away.

Dev was quick to note the implacable set of Pepper's jaw and decided it was past time to set the record straight. "I'm afraid the Ferrari belongs to the lady," he said, gesturing toward Pepper. "All rides are negotiated with her. She won't even let me drive it." He paused, then let a smile flicker. "I do, however, negotiate for my own beer. If the offer is still good, I'd be happy to join you."

He thought it strange that he didn't feel the pleasure at needling Pepper he'd been sure he would. He didn't want a beer and couldn't think why he'd agreed to accept one.

Patti and Sylvia each hurried to link an arm with his and move him toward the motor home. He shrugged them off, leaned back over the hood and snatched up his shirt, lunging to catch his belt before it hit the ground. He could hardly miss the triumphant smile Patti sent Pepper. Nor did the sudden crestfallen look Pepper gave in return escape him. It was almost enough to make him feel guilty for continuing this farce.

In fact, as Devlin left Pepper and followed the barracudas to their motor home, it occurred to him that his time might be better spent setting up his own camp and learning how to assemble the cot. He regretted the way he'd invited each malevolent dart shot by Pepper's eyes as he crossed the space between the two camps. That was why he insisted on staying outside the motor home to drink his beer, and why his pensive gaze followed Pepper's every move.

DETERMINED TO IGNORE the whole issue, Pepper exerted more energy than necessary doing camp chores. She cleaned the fire pit and laid a fire. She fed and watered Smedley, then grew angry when he loped over to Devlin and sat with his fuzzy head in Dev's lap.

Jealousy was a new emotion for her. It wasn't hard to recognize, just hard to handle. She didn't want to be jealous. *Wouldn't* be jealous, she sniffed. Especially of an officer. After all, that disgusting display with the women was the very behavior she'd expected from Devlin Wade. So why was she torturing herself? It was out of character for her to be moping around camp, envying the women whose laughter blended with his. It was also out of character for her to be wishing, deep down, that she was the one sharing his amusing stories.

Never one to sit idle long or to waste time feeling sorry for herself, Pepper decided to go fishing. She'd always loved the hour before dusk, that twilight time before night wrapped its dark cloak around her. Anticipating a mouth-watering meal of fresh fish cooked slowly over an open fire, she made short work of assembling rod and reel. She even whistled an aimless tune for Devlin's benefit.

HALF-HEARTEDLY, Devlin listened to Sylvia tell a funny story about an experience they'd had with the borrowed motor home, all the while wishing Pepper had invited him to go fishing. He envisioned sitting beside her on the vacant dock, the two of them talking quietly, maybe sharing tales of their travels. Two military brats ought to have quite a few stories to tell.

Suddenly he sat up straight, displacing the snoozing dog's head, wondering how such foreign thoughts had crept in. As he'd said to Pepper earlier, he didn't even like to fish. And look what listening to Candy Huston's tales of woe had netted him. Yet the vision of Pepper and him relaxing together remained vivid.

"Well, ladies," Dev drawled, draining his beer and getting up to throw the empty in the trash. "Thanks for the brew. It really hit the spot." He rubbed a lazy hand over his stomach. Patti followed the movement of his fingers unabashedly as he continued speaking. "However, if I don't call it quits, the alcohol, combined with heat I'm not accustomed to, well...it'll knock me on my tail." Stretching, Devlin yawned.

Patti rose, too, obviously keeping tabs on the ripple of muscles beneath his open shirt. "Come over for dinner later, why don't you?'' Once again, her fingers strayed to touch his chest.

Deftly he removed her hand. His eyes remained locked on Pepper's lone figure, fishing from the distant dock. His words were husky and absentminded. "With any luck, I'll be having fish for dinner."

The blonde turned to follow his gaze. "Business associate, huh?" She gave a knowing laugh. "I can see wife and five kids flashing from that look." She sighed. "Since the ring isn't on your finger, or through your nose, yet," she ventured with some sarcasm, "if you get tired of playing house before we eat, my offer for dinner is still open."

Unwillingly Dev pulled his gaze back. He brushed off Patti's invitation and stepped over the brunette in the lounge chair. "I'm sorry to disappoint you, but this really is a business trip. However, you're welcome to think what you like."

"Good enough, Major." Patti used the formality she'd found he was entitled to through a quick exchange of backgrounds earlier. Reaching out, she buttoned two buttons on Dev's shirt, cautioning, "I happen to think you'll strike out, so I'm conceding dinner and changing my offer to one of breakfast." Giving a coy wink that included her friend, she watched Devlin walk briskly away.

With a determined shake of his head, he turned, grinning, and tossed off a mock salute, then ran to catch up with Smedley. He slowed to a nonchalant saunter before reaching Pepper, seated with her feet hanging over the edge of the dock.

"So do we eat tonight, or what?"

His low growl rustled in Pepper's ear, startling her. She caught her breath, as she whirled to confront him, her fingers tightening around the fishing pole.

He was kneeling so close behind her that she could feel the warmth of his body and could smell the malt liquor on his breath. She had a sudden yearning to feel its biting taste on her own lips. A yearning so intense it frightened her. With firm denial, she pushed him away, erecting instead a barrier of antagonism.

"I told you before, we're separate, but equal." She held up two silvery fish for him to admire. "I've caught my dinner. Now you catch yours." Pepper jumped to her feet. "I'll even lend you my pole."

Taken by surprise, Dev grabbed for the pole, but lost it. It clattered to the dock and rolled very near the edge. Both reached to keep it from falling into the lake. Pepper caught it first, and a fraction of a second later, Dev's hand covered hers. Without removing his hand, he shoved the pole toward her. "You keep it," he said.

Smedley, who had stopped to sniff new territory along the path, loped over to join his human friends. Pepper, having fallen to one knee, remained there, stilled by the shock of their hands touching. The hand covered by Dev's rested loosely on the slippery pole.

Smedley chose to pounce just then, sending her tumbling headlong into Devlin,

Wavering backward and forward on one foot, he made a herculean effort to keep his balance. If he hadn't sensed her yearning—hadn't seen the moment she'd curbed her desire and backed away—maybe their touching wouldn't have made a difference to him. As it was, Smedley's nudge sent both of them crashing into the water. Man, woman, fish and pole landed in the shallow water amid Pepper's shrieks and Devlin's curses.

Dev was first to surface. He shook the water out of his eyes and looked for Pepper. The sun had recently dropped behind the ring of mountains, leaving the water around the dock murky. "Pepper!" he called, peering through the dark, choppy waves. His heart thundered in his ears. Then he saw her surface, and only then did he allow relieved laughter to break free.

Smedley stood on the dock, wriggling all over, cocking his head from side to side as if to question the sanity of the couple below. Choking and spitting water, Pepper was powerless to stop the dog's leap. She heard Devlin's laugh and took it to be at her expense. She failed to find a shred of humor in the situation that sent fish and pole into the churning wake of a small motorized raft heading for the opposite shore.

It wasn't that the water was deep, nor was it cold. Another time, Pepper might have found the dip and the romp with Smedley bracing. Now she just found it irritating. As the dog pounced from behind, she tumbled into the water again.

"Here, let me help you." Dev's boots settled on shifting sand as he tried sloshing through the water, intent on offering aid. Reaching out one hand to her, he lunged for Smedley's collar with the other.

The amusement in his voice was what prompted Pepper to strike his hand away. "I think you've helped quite enough, Major Wade. Thanks to your brand of help, I have no dinner. Neither do I have a pole to catch more fish. I'm glad you find it so hilarious. I don't." Shoving him aside, she pushed past, laboriously wading to shore.

Dev's feet slid. He tripped over Smedley and then the wake of another speeding rubber launch dashed him against the dock. His head struck the underpinnings with a solid thump. A bright array of stars flashed behind his eyes. He went under once and came up coughing.

Horrified by what her little display of temper had done, Pepper rushed to his side. "Dev—Major Wade!" She grasped his shirtfront. "I'm sorry. Are you all right?" She gazed worriedly into his pale face. Smedley, sensing the play was over, ambled toward shore, water flying every which way.

"I'm fine," Dev muttered, holding his head. "Between you and that mop of fur, I think I'll double my insurance, though."

Pepper wound her fingers more firmly into his ballooning khaki shirt, steadily pulling him toward shore. "It was all your fault," she scolded. "Serves you right for sneaking up on me like that." Sarcastically, she added, "What did you want anyhow? Did Barbie and her friend run out of beer?"

"Don't be nasty," admonished Dev, scrambling up the bank. Both were soaking wet and breathing hard. Smedley ran back and forth between them, yipping and shaking his wet fur, showering them with droplets of water. Dev's head was just beginning a dull ache.

If he'd thought Pepper's shirt had clung to her this morning, now it positively molded each and every curve. He knew it wasn't possible, but her satin shorts seemed to shrink even shorter while he watched. The desire he was starting to feel was the last thing he needed or wanted right now. And there was another reason for his irritation. An audience. Suddenly it seemed as if they were in the middle of a one-act play and all the other campers were watching them. Or did it just appear to him that the rising moon formed a spotlight and the fellow campers dotting the lakeshore were providing an audience for his and Pepper's real-life drama? Dev didn't know. He didn't care. What he did know was that he didn't want other men looking at this woman in her almost transparent shirt. Roughly he grabbed Pepper's arm and yanked her back toward their own camp.

She dug in her heels. "What on earth has gotten into you? Let go of me. If I can't catch more fish, we won't have any dinner."

Devlin's grip only tightened and he tugged harder. "You weren't planning on sharing anyway."

Smedley splattered water all over a group of bystanders. A sharp word from Devlin brought him to heel. Silence followed, until the dripping trio came to a standstill beside an unlit fire near Pepper's tent.

"Go change your clothes," Devlin ordered. "I'll start a fire to help dry your hair. Then we'll worry about food."

"Go to hell," Pepper spat, angered by his dictatorial manner. "I'm not one of your troops to be ordered about. And my hair is almost dry. You eat whatever you want, Major. Go eat with our neighbor, what's-her-name—"

"Patti," Devlin supplied. "With an 'i.'"

"Patti. That figures. Well, personally, I hope you choke on whatever you do eat. I'm going to bed." Dropping to her knees, Pepper crawled inside her tent. Smedley tried to wiggle in after, but she shoved him out.

In the ensuing silence, Devlin heard the door to the motor home slam. He heard Sylvia and Patti talking and smelled the enticing aroma of roasting wieners. He sat down heavily on the sand and began unlacing his soggy boots, cursing quietly.

"The offer for dinner still holds, Major," yelled Patti from somewhere within a halo of firelight.

Barefoot, Dev stood up and shucked off his wet shirt. He watched Smedley trot over to the neighbors begging food and saw Patti toss him two wieners in succession. "Thanks, but no," he called back. "And don't give the mutt too many of those things, or you can keep him for the night."

Inside her tent Pepper held her breath, waiting for Devlin to accept the offer. She cursed herself for acting childish and admitted to feeling her tension ebb when Dev refused Patti's invitation. She dropped her wet things in one corner of the small tent. If he wasn't an officer she'd be more remorseful, she thought, donning a cotton-knit teddy and sliding into the light sleeping bag covering her cot.

DEV SAT OUTSIDE watching each movement of Pepper's canvas tent. He hoped hunger pangs kept her awake all night. Lighting a fire, he paced until his fatigues dried. Surprisingly he was finding the night pleasant, the air warm and the stars brighter than he remembered ever having noticed before. The moon was large and golden, and the absence of city lights let him identify the North Star, the Big and Little Dippers, and other constellations with relative ease. As he was beginning to think this country might not be so bad after all, Patti crossed the open space between the two campsites. She carried a hot dog and another beer. Wordlessly she offered him both.

Arching one eyebrow, he accepted the hot dog, but waved off the beer, not caring to encourage Patti's company.

"Sylvia went to bed," Patti stated. "I'm not ready. Would you mind if we talk awhile?"

"You first," he suggested bluntly, biting into the juicy hot dog. "I'm not big on conversation just now."

She bobbed her gleaming cap of curls toward Pepper's darkened tent. "I just thought perhaps you were ready to admit I've won my bet. If you're tired of tantrums, I'm sure you and I could find a less…childish way to spend a moonlit evening."

Dev slowly chewed before swallowing the last bite. Tense again, he massaged the back of his neck. He accepted that times had changed and that women had an equal right to pursue, but he also recognized something a little old-fashioned in his own makeup. The part of him that resented Candy Huston's abuse of his friendship, and took offense at Gentleman Win's intrusion into his life, now found him resenting this outspoken woman's bold offer.

"Thanks for the food, Patti," he countered. "I really am out here solely to test a cot for the army. The minute this fire burns down, I damn well better get at it."

Again, barely discernible scuffling noises came from inside Pepper's tent. Dev knew full well that she was still awake and listening. Some perverse impulse made him wish he'd let Pepper stew, let her wonder if he intended sleeping alone. She might at least have the decency to give him credit for some scruples. Without fully understanding his own anger, he simply shook his head at Patti again.

"Well, good night then." The woman waved brusquely and, turning on her heel, lost no time in getting back to her own camp.

At least Patti was a graceful loser, and for that he was thankful, Dev thought, dumping the beer she'd left behind on the fire. It sizzled and steamed, immediately plunging his campsite into varying shades of gray and black. Only after he'd fumbled his way to the spot where he'd tossed his gear did Devlin remember that his cot was unassembled.

"Hell's bells," he grumbled. "Now the fire's stone cold and I'm left with this can of Tinkertoys to figure out by starlight." He sat down with the dark green tube and tried to catch a stray glimmer from a neighboring campfire. He'd be hanged if he'd ask Pepper for help, and he certainly couldn't invade Patti's well-lighted space after clearly shutting her out. Surely this thing came with instructions. He shook the tube. Netting was all that fell out.

PEPPER SHIFTED on her cot. She knew exactly what Devlin faced. Guilt dictated that she get up and at least offer to help him. Stubbornness held her prisoner where she lay. She strained to hear his muttered curses, knowing he'd never figure it out the first time without her help. Spitefully she thought, Major Boy-Wonder Wade was so gifted at solving puzzles, the cot should be a snap. After all, it was a simple-enough piece of equipment, invented by a woman, no less.

"Shame on you, Pepper Rivera," she whispered, turning her face away from Dev's muffled swearing. "A female chauvinist is just as bad as a male chauvinist."

Suddenly the tent flap snapped open. Pepper listened to a low scrape outside. Her heart rate accelerated, then subsided. It was only Smedley again, she decided. "Go away, Smedley," she hissed. "I told you before there isn't any room in here and I mean it—Oooh!" Her words ended in a squeal as her cot flipped up on edge and Pepper landed flat and hard on the packed sand. "Smedley..." she objected loudly, flailing a bare arm.

Devlin caught her upper arm and pinned her to the ground with his full length. "I'm damn sick of trying to match notches on that erector set you call a cot."

"You...you! Get out of my tent!" Pepper struggled to escape his grasp.

"So, the modern-day Annie Oakley has no room in her tent for man or beast?" Devlin's voice grated close to her ear and she could hear his caustic laughter, a low rumble in his chest.

"This ground is hard and lumpy," he whispered tightly. "Either we both sleep on a cot, Annie, or we both tough it out on the ground. Which will it be?"

"Get off me, you oaf." Pepper swung a free arm at him and missed. "What do you think you're doing? What if someone saw you come in here?" Her hand met air and shadows in the blackened tent. She couldn't see him, but he smelled of wood smoke, seaweed and a subtle scent that she'd decided just today must be uniquely Devlin Wade.

"And what makes you think I care?" He grabbed for her wrist again, furious now that he knew she'd been awake all along. He'd grown angrier by the minute, attempting to put her invention together by moonlight. And now...now he was downright mad. Still, when her sleeping bag fell open, Dev wasn't prepared to encounter Pepper's bare skin or her softness. The contact cooled his anger as effectively as if someone had thrown cold water in his face.

His breathing grew ragged, as one hand stroked a silken shoulder almost against his will. "What do you have on?"

"It's very warm tonight," she began, then stopped and shot back with hostility, "I'm decent if that's what has you bothered, Major. I wasn't planning on entertaining in my tent. And even if I were, you wouldn't have been invited." Pepper pushed against him, and under her hands grown suddenly weak, she felt Devlin's heated skin and solid muscle through the rough fabric of his shirt, a shirt dried stiff from his dunking in the lake.

"If it's so damn warm in here, why are you shivering?" Dev demanded, leaning closer, his fingers all but digging into her flesh. His lips came very close to hers. Close, but not quite touching.

Pepper froze, then found herself reaching—reaching up to explore his lips with one finger. Surprised at their trembling, she traced their soft shadowy outline with two fingers.

"Don't." Devlin turned his head to avoid her touch. Then uttering a short oath, he yanked her close again. "Yes! Yes..." His voice was steely, more determined the second time. "You've been taunting me...tempting me all day, lady. It's time we settled this once and for all."

Pepper's heart thudded wildly against her ribs. Her words tumbled end over end. "I'm sorry about your cot, Major. It's a simple-enough piece of equipment to assemble. I'll come out now and help—"

"The cot be damned," Devlin interrupted. His irritation had become explosive, his voice rough. Gravelly. And his mouth, when it closed over hers was meant to be rough, too. His intent was to take, to punish, to slake his longing with one kiss, so certain was he that one would be enough. But something about her answering hunger sent his intentions and his passion spiraling down and down into a fiery furnace—raging hot...hotter...hottest. The deeper Devlin Wade descended, the greater grew his need. And where he'd thought he wanted cool, thought he wanted sleek, thought he wanted sophisticated, he soon found that what he really wanted was all the hot spice sizzling just below the surface of Mary Kate Rivera.

Pepper hadn't expected Devlin's kiss—and it was the very unexpectedness that ignited untutored passions like the first stage of a rocket. She hurtled through second and third stages without knowing how to bank the flames from the forward thrust. Leveling out somewhere between heaven and earth, Pepper felt his kiss deepen until the very last measure of her cool exterior separated from her hidden, passionate core. No one had ever told her that kissing a man could resemble—surpass, even—a full-throttle ride in the Ferrari. And if she had to make a comparison, she'd consider this more like a lunar landing.

Devlin cupped her upturned face with both hands. How could he ever have thought one kiss would be enough? He wanted more. He wanted everything. A trickle of sweat ran slowly down his chest. The plastic edge of the cot nudged hard and cool at his back. The cot was firm. Real. And it was his only reason for being here, in her tent. For being on this trip at all.

Wasn't that also her reason? Self-condemning sanity came knocking at the logical portion of his brain. He closed the door solidly on desire and disengaged Pepper's arms.

"You'd hate yourself in the morning, Pepper...hate me, too." Devlin wanted to be gentle because he sensed her confusion and, with it, something more. He sensed her inexperience.

"Hate you?" Her voice floated in the darkness, dreamy...husky.

"If you didn't, your father certainly would." Dev used the first concrete reason he could think of, needing to put distance between them, not yet sure enough of his own control to relax his guard.

Pepper's head snapped up. Her cheeks burned from the sarcasm of his words. "What has my father got to do with us...with this...with anything?" she stammered.

He taunted her with what he guessed would make her angry. "I'm not looking to be drawn and quartered. So if you're harboring some idea of telling Daddy that I came here to seduce you, my advice is forget it. He has the reputation of being astute. He'd know I prefer women with more savvy."

Hurt took a quantum leap into outrage. Pepper gasped, clutching the cover of her sleeping bag protectively to her breasts. She wondered if Major Wade could hear the painful disintegration of her heart. She wondered, too, where she was lacking, what she'd done to warrant his spiteful accusation.

Fighting tears, Pepper gathered every shred of McTavish and Rivera pride she could muster. "My father believes you're honorable because you come from an honorable family, Major." Snatching up her own cot, she thrust it into Devlin's hands. "He would think you came to my tent for one reason only—a lesson on assembling the cot. I did hear Patti's offer and I'm sure she's a whole lot more savvy than I am." Her voice caught, almost broke as she clung to her dignity. "Hate won't wait until morning, Devlin Wade. I think I hate you now."

He told himself that making her hate him was all for the best, though her thinly veiled pain came close to unraveling what was left of his resolve. Not trusting himself to answer,

Dev took the cot she pushed at him and left her tent the same way he'd entered—in anger. Was she aware of what they'd almost lost tonight? His honor and her virtue. He doubted it.

But then again, maybe Pepper and his father were very much aware of the stakes on this outing. Dev promised himself that tomorrow he would go after the truth.

CHAPTER FIVE

Tuesday morning, Burro Peak, New Mexico

Rrring.

"Sheriff's Office. Oh, h'lo, Pop. What's new with you?

"You're plannin' what? Does Ruben know about this?

"What do you know about this dude, Pop? He's the son of an old army buddy? You call that a reference? Rube and I, well, we had someone else in mind.

"Yeah, Pop. I hear you. You want Pepper settled. You can be damn sure I'll check him out.

"Sure... Sure... Later."

Slam. Click.

ONCE PEPPER HAD WORKED through the initial stages of pain, resentment and rage, she sat cross-legged in her dark tent, locking together the scattered pieces of his cot, coldly and methodically analyzing the situation. What she decided was that men, as a whole, were no damn good. In that assessment, she included General Wyndom Wade for sending her on this nefarious excursion with his son, her father for giving it his blessing, and her brothers one and all, on the general principle that they were born male. Once she'd examined these generalities to her satisfaction and completed assembly of the cot, Pepper threw her sleeping bag haphazardly on the portable bed, savoring her condemnation of a very specific major.

Flinging herself down on the results of her handiwork, Pepper lay on her back staring into blackness. Her thoughts made a slow transition from wishing a hex on the major to reflecting on his kiss—that bone-melting, mind-bending kiss. A kiss, she was forced to admit, like none she'd ever experienced. She decided to forgive Dev Wade, partly because of that kiss, partly because they were stuck with one another's company and she didn't want to spend the next week feuding. She burrowed into her sleeping bag and fell into a restless sleep.

Sometime later, in the wee hours of the morning, Pepper was jarred from a very pleasant dream by the sound of a dog barking. She didn't want to leave her dream state, and it was only after hearing angry voices, one of them loudly cursing a "stupid sheepdog" that Pepper bolted upright, Smedley's name a nagging whisper in her sleep-dulled brain.

She sat for a moment, rubbing her eyes with both fists, but instead of fading, the commotion grew progressively louder. Pepper scrambled off the cot, digging around in the dark for the shorts she'd tossed in the corner. She tugged them on and crawled from the tent to check out the source of trouble. Just as she'd first suspected, Smedley was in the thick of it.

When she finally corralled him, he was leaping and barking at the base of a spindly ponderosa pine. Perched high on a limb above his head was a hissing cat, whose tail was doubled in size from fear. Each time the cat yowled, Smedley lunged and barked excitedly.

The cat owners lit into Pepper the minute her hand closed over the errant dog's collar. And they weren't appeased by her apology. They were furious.

"Bad dog," she scolded, after managing to escape the irate couple and after she'd manhandled all fifty pounds of dog back to her own site. "Don't you know how expensive a Maine Coon cat is, Smedley?" she admonished, mimicking the stern and snobbish owners.

Pepper dragged a short length of rope out of her backpack and, in between yawns, tied the dog tightly to a stunted piñon tree. "There," she promised, "that should hold you until daylight, my fuzzy friend. And you can really consider yourself in the doghouse now. First, you lost my fish, then you harrassed that poor cat."

Smedley licked her face. An indulgent smile touched Pepper's lips involuntarily and stayed there until it was supplanted by another wide yawn. "Well, I'm going to try to catch another forty winks," she murmured, giving him a final pat. "See that you behave."

As Pepper returned to her tent, the moon slid out from behind a cloud, illuminating Devlin's campsite. For the first time since she'd awakened, she wondered how he'd managed to sleep through the noise. He must sleep like a log, she mused, hiding yet another yawn behind an open palm. It was quite by chance that she saw a light go on, then off again, in the motor home. Perhaps he'd taken that woman up on her offer, after all. If so, Smedley's ruckus wouldn't have been nearly as loud through the walls of the giant conveyance, Pepper guessed.

It gave her something to think about as she crawled into her sleeping bag, only to be vividly reminded that the dream she'd so reluctantly interrupted had centered on Devlin Wade.

Not more than an hour later she was awakened by a rude demand. "Pepper... Pepper Rivera! Get up and come out here. Now!" Devlin stood outside her tent, yelling. Giving orders.

She stuck a tousled head through the flap and, blinking into the bright sun, frowned up at him.

But he wasn't paying attention to her. He was holding Smedley by the collar and talking to a tall man wearing cotton chinos. Pepper quickly withdrew from sight and dressed in yesterday's clothes. She arrived outside in time to catch the men's final handshake.

"Someone you know?" she asked, as she stared after the older man's retreating form. She was slightly nervous, wondering how she should act around Devlin today.

His tone barely civil, Devlin answered her question with another. "Is it normal for you to be evicted from a campground?"

Pepper shot a look at Smedley, remembering the cat. Anxiously her gaze returned to meet Devlin's scowl. Trying to appear as casual as possible, she leaned down, rummaged in her backpack and pulled out two oranges. Hesitantly she offered Devlin one. "Here, you'll probably feel better if you eat something. I'm usually edgy before breakfast, too. I'll hike over to the little store later and pick up something for a real meal."

"I never eat breakfast," he said shortly, passing one hand over an unshaven jaw. "If you can keep your damn dog under control for fifteen minutes, I'd like to shower and shave."

"What's he doing loose?" she blurted. "Did you untie him?"

Smedley's tail thumped expectantly on the ground. He whined, tugging against Devlin's tight grip. Devlin curtly ordered the dog to sit, then picked up two pieces of rope and thrust them under her nose.

"It broke?"

"Chewed," he spat. "That man you saw here is the manager of the campground. It seems he's had several complaints about *your* dog. Do you understand? The manager is asking you to leave."

"He's not *my* dog." Pepper's temper flared, then her tone changed as she eyed Smedley balefully. "But he is my responsibility."

She grinned, tossing one orange nonchalantly in the air, then catching it with ease, as she spoke. "I have to agree he's totally truant. You should have seen him square off with Garfield just before daybreak. It was total bedlam around here for over an hour. He woke up half the campers. I'm surprised you slept through it. You must have found my cot satisfactory, Major." Pepper was fishing, knew it, and didn't like it. Still, she thought he might brag if he'd spent the time with the neighbor.

All he did, however, was loop the longer end of the rope through Smedley's collar and tie him securely to the tree again. Then pulling a dufflebag from the Ferrari, he calmly unzipped it.

"My brother, Miguel, lives over near Burro Peak. It's not far, so we may as well head his way," Pepper ventured.

Dev lifted an eyebrow and grunted. "Suit yourself." Hauling out his shaving kit, skivvies and another set of fatigues, he turned and sauntered toward the showers.

Heat rose in Pepper's cheeks. She felt like throwing one of her oranges at him. She wondered if her aim was still as accurate as it used to be when she played baseball with her brothers. After all, she needed a shower and a change of clothing, too. Devlin made it sound as though he were in charge here, making rules and assigning duties. And she was obviously assigned to Smedley patrol.

She brushed a hand over the wrinkled satin shorts, now dulled and stiffened with sand from the dirty lake. "Do you suppose his Majorship is always this surly in the morning, Smedley? Or do I just bring out the worst in him?"

Smedley barked twice, lunging toward her only to be pulled up short on his tether. His bark turned into a surprised yelp. As Pepper knelt to rub his ears, he pounced, toppling her.

She had to laugh, and some of her good humor was restored. "Good thing for you, you mangy mop, that these shorts are already dirty." She was inspecting her equally disreputable-looking shirt when Patti descended the steps of the motor home wearing dazzling white shorts, her hair perfectly washed and curled. And it didn't help matters that Patti chose to drink her morning coffee elegantly poised in the chair where Devlin had drunk his beer the night before.

Patti smiled knowingly.

Seething, without knowing precisely why, Pepper unleashed Smedley and headed for the lakeshore at a brisk trot. Exercise always let her see things with a clearer eye, and she broke into a flat-out run. She would ignore Patti and purge her mind of Major Wade. Throughout her run, Pepper worked on convincing herself that she didn't need a man. What she needed was a life of her own—no masculine interference. It made sense.

When she returned from her self-imposed torture, Pepper's legs were trembling and she was sweating profusely, despite the early hour. Smedley's tongue was hanging out and he drank thirstily of the water she set out for him. Only after she'd given him a bowl full of food did Pepper see that Devlin had already returned from his shower. Meticulous and in combat gear again, he stood casually, one foot resting on a chair, sharing coffee with Perfect Patti.

Pepper's heart plunged to her toes. All her hard-won convictions were in danger of vanishing the instant her eyes connected with a freshly showered, newly shaved, Major Devlin Wade. Her knees almost let her down. *Blast the man for being so cool.* Solemnly Pepper gathered clean clothing and used every ounce of remaining strength to drag herself off to the showers. Did Perfect Patti ever sweat? she wondered.

As heat from the spray hit her in the face, Pepper's recently acquired good sense tilted and slid away. It hurt to see Devlin acting so easy and nonchalant with the other woman.

Pepper pulled herself up short with a reminder that not only was Major Wade an officer, he didn't like animals. He hated her car, he didn't like camping, and if she wanted to get picky, she had a host of other charges mounting against him. There was no question in her mind; the two of them were definitely unsuited! Yet by the time she'd changed into clean purple shorts and a gold tank top, she was ready to admit that she was intrigued by him in a way she'd never been intrigued by any man before. The difficulty was in knowing what to do about it.

Quietly she set about breaking camp, wondering how she was going to get through the next week.

SEATED IN THE ENEMY CAMP, Dev knew he should help pack. He chastised himself for staying, but also knew if he took one step toward Pepper feeling the way he did right now, he'd likely do something not becoming an officer and a gentleman. The vibrancy of her color combinations excited him, as did the curve of her cheek and the fiery red-gold of her hair. He thought about calling his father and telling him there was no contest, that the general had won this round, hands down. However, he didn't move from Patti's chair, because he'd forced himself to remember his first order of business—clearing his name.

"You haven't heard a word I'm saying," Patti chided.

Devlin drifted out of a fog. "Uh, thanks for the java," he muttered, flushing guiltily. "I don't think I'd have made it through the morning without it." As an afterthought, he added, "Hey, I hope things work out for you and Sylvia on this trip."

Patti remarked wryly, "I wish I could say the same for you, and mean it." She chuckled. "Why, Major, I do believe your business partner is about to dissolve your partnership."

Her laugh shook him from his stupor. Dev leaped to his feet. Pepper and Smedley were already seated in the Ferrari and she had just started the engine. Throwing Patti an impersonal salute, Dev raced through the campsite, jerked open the passenger door and climbed in beside Pepper.

Ignoring him, she calmly shifted into reverse. "Next time we break camp," she said pointedly, "if you plan on riding with me, you'd better stow your own gear, or you can hitchhike back to get it. You might not find anyone as accommodating at our next campsite." She inclined her head toward a smirking Patti.

Connecting his seat belt, Dev settled back into the leather upholstery and tipped his khaki cap over his eyes, studying her guardedly. "Lady, you want my help, ask for it. I offered to help last night and you refused. I don't ask twice." The Ferrari had made its first bump onto the main road before he added, as if surprised, "Your cot was more comfortable than I expected. How did you happen to come up with an idea like that?"

She smiled, now that she'd learned where he spent the night. "Would you believe it was spawned by an unconquerable fear I have of sharing my sleeping bag with some creepy-crawly?"

"Nah!" Devlin opened an eye to peer out from under his cap. "A tough lady like you? You could've fooled me. But that still doesn't tell me how a person invents something."

She glanced sharply at him to see if he was poking fun. Seeing nothing in his clear blue eyes except honest interest, she relaxed against the seat and answered, "I was the only girl in a family of five athletic boys. I wanted to play football like they did. My father thought it would be more appropriate for me to take up art." She shrugged. "My artistic ability was limited to the basics—my mind preferred the strategy of football. And inventing's mostly a matter of identifying problems and working out strategies to get around them. Did you think all inventors were well-trained scientists?"

He was looking at her lips as she spoke. "I don't know. I've never known an inventor."

Flustered, Pepper averted her gaze. "It helps to have time on your hands. The men who visited Papa were always talking about what they needed in the field. The hard part is getting a patent. That takes patience and research—the real secret of the trade."

"Sounds fascinating." Dev waited, wondering if she'd said all she was going to say on the subject. He had to admit it; he found *her* fascinating. She was unpredictable. She was also the daughter of a general. He pulled his hat lower over his eyes. A wiser avenue for him would be to take a nap.

Pepper knew when Devlin's erratic breathing evened out and he'd fallen asleep. "He's got some nerve," she groused to Smedley, who'd also hunkered down for a snooze. "Both of you have some nerve," she finished, taking a sharp corner at a fast clip. "I'm the one who was up half the night chasing a dog! Uh-oh." She whistled low through her teeth. A police car had pulled in behind her from a side road and the officer had flipped on his flashing reds.

Pepper eased into the first lay-by. They'd been climbing steadily into the Mogollon mountains after leaving Caballo Lake, the roadway a narrow, two-lane track with barely any other traffic. As she relaxed, she'd been gradually increasing her speed. Now she prayed the major would stay asleep. She didn't need his I-told-you-so, since he'd already accused her of trying to qualify for the Daytona 500 yesterday.

Grabbing her handbag, Pepper jumped out to meet the approaching lawman. She wondered how close she was to her brother's territory. This was something she'd rather Miguel didn't know about.

"Is something wrong, Officer?" she asked, flashing him a warm smile, fully aware that she'd been exceeding the speed limit by a good ten miles an hour.

Removing his hat, the man grinned back. Unabashedly his eyes admired the length of her bare leg, then switched to the Ferrari. "You own this powerhouse?" he asked as he pulled out his ticket book and walked behind to view her license plates.

"Why, yes I do," she admitted nervously, chewing at her lower lip. She'd never had a ticket before. He began to scribble on his pad.

"You wanna wake up Rip Van Winkle over there?" The officer nodded toward Dev's slumped form.

"No!" It came out sharper than Pepper had intended. "I mean," she faltered, "I own the car. Why do you need him?" She pulled out her driver's license and handed it to the patrolman.

"Had a bank robbery over in Elephant Butte earlier today. Two suspects got away in a red car. Rivera, huh? Any relation to—"

Pepper rushed her words, cutting off his question. "Surely you don't think I . . . we—" she broke off stammering, as Dev scrambled from the car, sleepily rubbing his eyes. "Major!" Her voice sounded strained. "This man thinks we robbed a bank."

Taking in the twinkle in the young officer's eye, Dev paused a moment to stretch. "I wondered how the lady could afford this car, Officer," he joked. "She claims to be an inventor. Obviously a lie. Looks more like a gun moll to me. You won't find my fingerprints on that steering wheel. I just hitched a ride." He smiled guilelessly.

"Major Wade!" Pepper stared at him, open-mouthed. She hadn't pegged him as the type to joke, but catching the wink he aimed at the officer, her shock turned to sputtering indignation. "Oh, you men in uniform are all alike. Pompous and overbearing." She snatched her license back, glaring at Devlin across the roof of the car.

"Watch it," warned the young policeman teasingly, still giving Pepper and her car a covetous glance. "Insult an officer of the law and the price of speeding goes up."

Pepper compressed her lips, standing silently while he wrote the ticket. She seethed, while the two men chatted amicably. When the ticket and a lecture on speeding had been delivered, the officer returned to his car, throwing Dev a mocking salute.

"Didn't I warn you yesterday that you had a lead foot?" He calmly opened Pepper's door and doffed his cap.

"Don't start on me," she said crossly. "It's your turn to drive and my turn to sleep. We'll see if you can keep it under the limit here." Pepper marched past him and climbed into the passenger seat. "And I don't need any comments from you, either," she snapped at Smedley as he raised a sleepy head and whined.

"What's the matter? Didn't get your beauty sleep last night?" Dev's tone was wickedly challenging even though he knew he should let well enough alone. Suddenly he felt gloriously alive. It was cooler in the mountains now with the sun filtering through a thicket of sugar pine. He'd awakened relaxed, and to be truthful, he'd enjoyed seeing Pepper squirm. Out here in the wilderness she seemed so self-possessed. It did his heart good to see something rattle her. He grinned, folding his long legs under the steering wheel.

Ignoring him, Pepper pulled a pillow from the cramped space beside Smedley. Plumping it to her satisfaction, she molded it around her neck, then closed her eyes.

Dev started the car. "Will I know when we get to your brother's?" He ran his tongue over dry lips, giving her purple shorts a skeptical once-over. "Will he have a psychedelic, neon sign spelling out Rivera? Or is the rest of your family more conventional?"

Pepper opened one eye. "Miguel? Conventional?" She gave a snort of laughter. "Never." Snuggling back into the seat, Pepper wondered what her renegade brother, the only county sheriff she knew whose black leather jacket said "Sweet Harley" on the back, would think of a spit-and-polish West Pointer like Devlin Wade. Closing her eyes again, she turned away from him. "You can't get lost," she mumbled around a yawn. "The road runs out at Burro Peak." Within minutes she was asleep.

Deep in contemplation, Dev cruised along comfortably while Pepper snoozed. He let one arm hang loosely outside the window, and opened his shirt, inviting the cool mountain breeze to dry his damp chest. He was actually enjoying the drive through the lonely Gila wilderness, thinking that the next town they hit, he'd buy himself some cotton shorts and shirts. He slid a cassette into the tape deck and was pleasantly surprised to hear Rachmaninoff. Devlin glanced at Pepper—she was full of surprises.

A lawman on a motorcycle roared past in the opposite direction. Slowing, he blew a siren, lit his red beacon and made a U-turn. Abruptly a thick arm lifted, motioning Devlin to stop.

Caught off guard, Dev quickly checked his speed, confirming that he was under the limit. He sighed in exasperation, slowing before he came to a full stop. It had to be this blasted red car, he reasoned. Rural police had probably never seen anything like it. He shot a quick glance at Pepper, who was showing signs of waking, and reached in his hip pocket to remove his wallet, preparing for the inevitable—and for her retaliation after his own earlier heckling. A silent oath died on his lips as he glanced up to see a bear of a man approaching the Ferrari.

The sheriff was tall, with wide shoulders, and generally resembled a tank. He had jet-black hair that brushed a standup collar. A polished leather headband matched the gleam of high-topped boots. "Damn," Dev exclaimed under his breath. "Does it have to be Rambo?"

Still caught up in his horrified survey of the tough-looking cop, Devlin heard but didn't grasp Pepper's squeal of delight. Nor did he comprehend when he saw Pepper flying from the car to throw herself into the big man's arms.

Smedley awakened with a start, baring his teeth and growling low in his throat. It was all Dev could manage to haul the animal away from the window. Even then it took some doing to extricate himself from the car while preventing Smedley's escape. When he did succeed, he saw Pepper, her arms looped around the sheriff's waist, chattering like a magpie. Apparently immune to Pepper's chatter, the burly man nailed Devlin with a look that said he might well be some slimy new specimen under a microscope.

"Mike, I'd like you to meet Major Devlin Wade." Pepper tugged the reluctant sheriff a step closer. "Devlin, this is my brother, Miguel, but we sometimes call him Mike." She grinned happily, oblivious to the fact that the men were eyeing each other warily.

Mike was first to extend his hand, though grudgingly, and his bone-crushing handshake numbed Dev's fingers. Dev didn't drop his gaze or wince, although that required real effort.

"Why did you pull me over, Sheriff?" His question was blunt, laced with resentment.

Mike scowled, pausing to glance at Pepper. "Pop called. He told me Pepper was headed this way. Pete clued me in about those vanity plates. They'd be hard to miss."

"Why did Pop call?" Pepper asked, annoyed. "I didn't give him any arrival time, because Devlin and I are testing my cot."

"Oh?" Mike's tone was frigid.

"My invention. We're testing it." Mike still glared at Devlin. "Separately, silly." Pepper punched her brother's arm, then lowered her eyes, studying her toes in embarrassment. At that exact moment, Dev wiggled his first two fingers and stated firmly, "Two cots, Sheriff. One each."

"Uh-huh," Mike grunted, crossing his arms, examining Devlin no less skeptically. "Well, now...if we hustle, Maria will have enough warning to make a bigger pan of enchiladas. You are spending the night?"

Pepper yawned around an answer. "We sure will. I didn't sleep much last night. I'm looking to turn in early."

"Something keep you up last night?" Miguel shot the question at Pepper, but his eyes locked on Dev.

She blushed, glancing from one man to the other. "Nothing special. Just the usual first night on the road...dog problems...the heat. Oh, the air conditioner quit in the Ferrari. I'm counting on you to fix it." Looping an arm through Mike's, she avoided looking at Dev.

"Sure, kid." Mike opened the car door, handing Pepper in. "Follow me," he ordered Dev tersely. "And don't run over me with all that horsepower."

Dev sucked in his breath. He didn't relish spending an hour, let alone an evening, with Miguel Rivera, and he told Pepper so as soon as they were alone. "I have the distinct feeling your brother wouldn't mind having me shot at sunrise."

"Oh, come on. Don't be that way," she chided. "He isn't usually this rude. I can't imagine why he wouldn't like you."

Pepper spoke calmly and matter-of-factly as Dev continued to scowl. Somehow she'd forgotten that she'd vowed not to like the Major herself. "I want to show you some of the countryside tomorrow," she went on,. "The old Santa Rita open-pit copper mine is just a few minutes' drive from Mike's ranch. They have an interesting tour. Wait and see, you two will be best of friends by the time dinner's over."

By the time Dev had suffered through a silent dinner, he didn't think more erroneous words were ever uttered. Well, not really silent, he admitted stoically. Pepper and Miguel's wife, Maria, chattered nonstop. Only Miguel was silent. He answered Dev's questions in words of one syllable, if he chose to answer at all. Even before the coffee was served, Dev had stopped trying.

At the first opportunity after the dishes were done, Devlin grabbed Pepper by the arm. "I want to leave."

She stubbornly held her ground. "Wouldn't you like to sleep inside on a bed tonight? Alone," she added, blushing when Dev lifted a brow suggestively.

"No to both," he responded. "But if we do stay, I insist we sleep outside on your cots. After all, isn't that the only reason for our making this fun little side trip?" Blue eyes glittered at her under the light of the bug blaster.

"All right, Major," she agreed. "You find out where Mike wants us to set up camp. I plan to talk with Maria awhile. I don't get over this way very often."

"You do that." Dev snorted derisively. "Big brother will probably tie you to the bedpost and direct me into the next county with an armed escort."

"That's pure nonsense, Major Wade. He doesn't know anything about you. Why would my brother mistrust you?"

Dev's fingers closed around her upper arm. "You don't trust me, either, Pepper, and I'd like to know the real reason. You spit out *Major* like it's a dirty word, even if that kiss you delivered last night said something quite different."

Pepper shook off his hand. "I didn't deliver anything, Major—you took! And I've lived on a military post all my life, long enough to know that not all Majors are worthy of trust." Her chin tilted and she gave him a frosty look. "I don't know what you hoped to prove with your kiss, Devlin Wade, but I don't think you want to flaunt it here. You might do well to know that Miguel is a little hotheaded. He's always been overprotective of me." She drew shamelessly on her brother's reputation now that she was backed into a corner—backed in tight, and terrified of letting Devlin see how his kiss had really affected her. Her chin rose higher. "Don't bother to wait up for me, Major. I'll give you a head start on testing your cot tonight. And I can assure you, we're both lucky Miguel doesn't think we're doing anything other than testing them. Otherwise we'd be posting banns tomorrow. Miguel just looks like an easy rider. Believe me, he's traditional through and through."

"Whew!" Dev stepped back as Pepper stalked into the kitchen, slamming the screen door on the last of her scathing delivery. He'd been so absorbed by the fiery passion of her eloquence, he hadn't listened to her threat. Right now his eyes burned, his head ached, and nothing she'd said made sense. He just knew he didn't want to spar with her until he could be surer of his footing.

He walked to the edge of Miguel's front porch and leaned against a Joshua tree, enjoying its solid strength, as he let his mind drift aimlessly. He stared up at the sky with its smattering of clouds wrapping feathery fingers around a crescent moon. Smedley padded nearby, his identification tags clinking softly as he sniffed at low-growing sage.

The pungent odor of freshly lit tobacco wafted past Dev's nose. He squinted into the darkness, making out the thickset form of Mike Rivera by the small flame of the match he still held.

"Pepper tells me you've both decided against staying in the house tonight." The smell of sulfur overpowered the tobacco as Mike deliberately snuffed out his match.

Devlin's eyes adjusted to the blackness again. He shrugged, sounding more relaxed than he felt. "I can't truthfully recommend Pepper's cot to the army if I spend my nights in a feather bed, now can I?"

Silence stretched between them as each took the other's measure. Miguel's grunt, when it came, might have been agreement. At the very least, Dev took it as reluctant acceptance.

"Get your gear, Major. I'll take you down by the lake to set up camp. When the sun breaks over Burro Peak in the morning, you'll see something most city folk don't ever get to witness."

Dev smiled wryly. So the sheriff was going to make an effort to atone for his rudeness? Well, maybe if he got to know her family, he'd begin to understand Pepper better.

Devlin bent to hoist his pack and Pepper's. "Beautiful sunrise, huh?" he asked Miguel companionably.

"Like something out of history, *amigo*. You'll see." One flick of a powerful flashlight, and Mike illuminated a narrow trail. He not only relieved Dev of Pepper's compact pack, but stayed until their camp was set up to his liking.

Even after his host left, Dev had every intention of waiting up to discuss a few things with Pepper. Yet Smedley's soft snoring, as he slept near the hypnotically dancing campfire, soon had Devlin nodding off. Deciding his talk with Pepper could wait until morning, he turned in for the night.

PEPPER SWAPPED STORIES with her sister-in-law until the tired old grandfather clock in the living room struck 2 a.m. "Mike went to bed hours ago," Pepper said to Maria around a yawn. "He won't ask me to visit again, I'm afraid, keeping you up this way."

Maria struggled to open her heavy-lidded eyes. "That reminds me, Pepper. The trail to the lake is spooky at night. No telling what kind of polecats are out. Let me at least find you a flashlight. I don't know why Mike is having you camp clear down by the lake. There's a big powwow setting up near the lake tonight. Starts tomorrow. Are you sure you won't change your mind and stay the night inside?"

"There's nothing out on the trail for me to fear. A powwow, huh? I wonder if Mike told Major Wade. He's from the East, you know. I doubt they have ceremonial powwows in Washington." Giving her overanxious sister-in-law a reassuring hug, Pepper left, using a stray moonbeam to illuminate the steep trail. She'd make a point of getting up before Devlin in the morning, so she could fill him in on what to expect.

CHAPTER SIX

DEV AWAKENED SLOWLY at dawn's first blush. He stretched and shivered in the cool morning air, surprised to have slept so soundly. He couldn't wait to see Pepper's face when she learned that he'd put together not only his own cot, but hers. And in mere minutes yet. When he saw no sign of stirring in her tent it crossed his mind that she might have stayed at the house, after all. Restless, yet reluctant to check her tent, considering what had happened the first evening, Devlin decided to take Smedley for a quick run.

A ghostly white mist was rising from the lake when he and the dog returned, both panting from their exertions. The smooth sheen of crystalline water offered the promise of cooling him down quickly. Standing by the water's edge, Dev surveyed the area and considered skinny-dipping—not something a major in the U.S. Army would normally do. He chuckled. It was clearly proof that he was already thinking of himself as a civilian. Completely satisfied that there was still no movement from Pepper's tent, Devlin stripped and plunged naked into a lake so cold it made his toes curl and his teeth chatter.

To keep his blood circulating as he stood in waist-deep water, Devlin grabbed a nearby floating stick and tossed it up on the shore, tempting the dog to chase it. Drawn into the game, Smedley retrieved the stick and splashed into the water with it, into a deeper area that forced Dev to dive if he wanted to continue the game. Surfacing, Dev shook wet hair from his eyes, imitating the dog, who was already wading back to shore, the stick forgotten.

As he started to follow the dog, a movement on shore caught Dev's attention. Dismayed, he watched a band of perhaps five young Native Americans in feathered headbands race down a nearby slope toward the lake. He blinked away the water, fully expecting the mirage to disappear. The boisterous group continued to advance.

Barking wildly, Smedley ran in circles. Abruptly he loped off toward camp, still barking. Shivering, Dev stood in the waist-deep water, quietly gaping.

"Uncle Zach. Uncle Zach." A small voice penetrated his foggy haze. "What should we do now? There isn't supposed to be a man or a dog in our lake, is there?"

Feeling curiously as though he'd drifted into another century, Dev watched the boys, hardly a one over the age of twelve, cluster around a tall man dressed head to toe in buckskin—a man who seemed inordinately interested in Dev's invasion of the lake.

"Well, as I live and breathe, is it really Devlin Wade? What the devil are you doing in New Mexico, you old son-of-a-gun?"

Bouncing to keep warm, Dev scrubbed water from his eyes, thinking he'd heard the mirage in buckskin shout his name. Uppermost in his mind was getting to shore and reaching his pants. But when Dev took a closer look at the wearer of those fringed, knee-high moccasins, he was shocked to see someone familiar.

"Zachary Mankiller?" Dev's genuine surprise rose above the cacophony of Smedley's barking. Seeing the other's nod of agreement, Devlin threw back his head and laughed. "I always figured things were getting tough in Washington, but really, Zach... A hotshot, Harvard attorney like yourself. What's Congress up to this time? No, don't tell me, let me guess. We've discovered oil in this vast wilderness and you've been sent here to foreclose on the property."

Also laughing, the newcomer sloshed through the water, stretching out a welcoming hand, dousing his tan buckskins. "You're a fine one to talk, Wade." A grin softened the hawk-sharp features. "You, standing here in this freezing water naked as a jaybird. Is this some new ritual for the Pentagon?" Turning serious, Zach added, "Once a year, I lend a hand at my tribe's ceremonial powwow. Not only does it help me keep Washington in perspective, but at the same time it keeps an important part of our culture alive for the kids. But you... Major Wade, what brings the Playboy of the Pentagon to these desolate parts?"

Before Dev had a chance to launch into his story—he had ceased to notice how cold the water was—they were interrupted. "Uncle Zach! Uncle Zach!" A plaintive cry ended on a warning note that had both Zach and Dev whipping their heads around.

"Holy Moly! Get back everyone." Zach's jaw went slack. He shifted toward Dev.

"Geez, Pepper." Dev hissed her name as a constricting breath closed his throat. He took a step toward shore, then stopped to stare. Barefoot, Pepper stood on the bank of the lake in a thigh-length nightshirt. With red hair in a tangled riot of curls, she looked as though she'd just stepped from a warm bed. Dev didn't think he'd ever seen her look more bewitching. But Pepper wasn't the reason for his and Zach's distress. The reason was Smedley—or rather Smedley and the mother skunk and two babies he was chasing out of the underbrush behind Pepper. And Smedley was bouncing and wiggling the way he always did when he thought he'd found a friend.

Dev stood shivering and watching. Inexperienced though he was in such matters, he was sure that if the arch of Mama Skunk's tail was any indication, she wasn't about to be Smedley's friend.

Turning to see what the men were staring at, Pepper clapped her hands together sharply and ordered, "Smedley, leave that skunk alone." The dog bounded to her side, barking. "Devlin," she asked in a husky early-morning voice, "are you all right? What's going on here?" Her questioning gaze took in Zach and the boys.

But before Devlin could introduce Zach, Smedley dashed away, ending nose to nose with the waddling baby skunks. And Mama wasn't pleased.

"Oh no! Smedley. Smedleeee!" Pepper leaped for the water's edge just as Mama took aim and sprayed. Smedley yelped in surprise. Zach dived for deeper water and Devlin lunged toward shore, intent only on helping Pepper.

She raced toward Devlin, keeping him in her sights until the sun's rays breaking through the rising mists bathed his form in glittering gold, almost blinding her. His broad shoulders blocked the sun, and for Pepper, it was like watching a Greek god rising from the sea. Wordlessly, she stared, until it registered that Dev didn't have a stitch on. As heat rose to her cheeks, driving the numbness away, she stumbled on a ridge and pitched face forward in the shallow water.

Devlin hauled her, sputtering, to the surface. She was all soft wet curves, where he was frozen rigid muscle. He paused. For just a moment, their warm breath mingled. He watched the pulse in her throat slam alarmingly, erratically, and his matched.

Seeking to recover a balance, he tore his gaze away. For the first time, he noticed the upper hillside, dotted everywhere with tepees. A circle of silent onlookers had formed around them. And down a nearer bank, Pepper's brother charged, like a Sherman tank. The man was bare of foot, bare of chest and strapping on a no-nonsense side arm.

Pepper had just begun to struggle in Dev's embrace. He hauled her into deeper water, making an effort to avoid her swinging arm, but she accidentally caught him a blow to the midriff. He swallowed a mouthful of lake water and commenced coughing.

Holding Pepper at bay, Dev saw Zach's young troops take cover in the lake, complaining about the biting, acrid skunk smell on shore. A yipping, howling Smedley, scrubbing at the shaggy fur around his hidden eyes, created greater pandemonium by following the boys into the water.

Suddenly Zachary Mankiller's deep laugh sliced cleanly through the rising mists, followed by his mocking words. "And to think I discounted all those rumors floating around D.C. concerning your disappearance, Wade. I thought I knew you better. Care to tell the whole truth and nothing but the truth?"

"Dammit, Zach!" Dev splashed water at his old friend with the flat of his hand. "I'd like nothing better than to tell somebody the truth about what happened in D.C. But just now we've got trouble of another brand."

Zach turned toward the shore to follow Dev's gaze. His grin faded as he found himself staring at the unshaven, unkempt and very angry Miguel Rivera.

"You just wanna step aside, Mankiller, and let my sister come out?" The sheriff's tone sounded deadly, and as yet, Mike was upwind from the retreating skunk family. Dev couldn't wait to see the grouchy sheriff when he got a good whiff.

"Your sister?" Zach's voice was incredulous. He whirled around, taking another look at the woman struggling in Dev's loose hold. She had a hand covering her nose, but her emerald eyes were as big as saucers. With long red hair plastered close to her head, she showed little resemblance to the swarthy Miguel. "Whatever you say, Mike." Zach waded to the bank. "Hey, you kids," he yelled at his young charges. "You guys grab the dog. Take him to Luke's mom. Round up every can of tomato juice you can find and give him a bath in it. That should neutralize the smell and stop his pain. Hurry it up. After that, you can burn your clothes and take a bath yourselves." Only after Zach threatened to fail every last one of them did the boys do as he asked.

Miguel grunted. "Pepper, get up here and tell me what all this racket is about. Then maybe the good folks on the bank can get back to their business."

Pepper stared at him a moment. Turning, she checked on Dev, pausing to rake the wet hair away from her still-flushed face.

Dev's heart thundered against his rib cage. It seemed to him that everything Pepper Rivera did attracted a crowd. And now, as she had at Caballo Lake, she managed to look just innocent enough to raise his protective hackles. His fingers tightened around her arm. Something made him resent the way Miguel was tossing out orders.

"Why don't the lot of you just trot right out of that lake and somebody can tell me what's goin' on." Miguel walked to the water's edge. "Maybe you, Zach. You, I know, have good sense. Yuck! What smells like skunk?" Miguel backed away holding his nose.

"Skunk." Pepper pulled out of Dev's hold and sloshed through the water, stopping to glare up at a scowling Miguel. He snatched her wrist and dashed quickly upwind again.

Dev refused to leave the water despite Miguel's insistence. He'd be damned if he'd stand dressed in his altogether to be judged by Mike Rivera, or anybody else, with Pepper looking on. He crossed his arms and scowled back, clamping his mouth shut to keep from breathing the foul air now reaching over the water.

Pepper tugged free of Miguel. "Devlin must be freezing," she said. "He's not wearing anything."

Mike's head jerked up. "Is that right, Major? You out there skinny-dippin' where my little sister has a ringside seat?"

"Oh, ye gods, Mike!" Pepper threw up her hands. "I'm twenty-five years old." Angry color spilled into her cheeks as she confronted the blustering sheriff. "When are you going to stop this macho act you put on and admit I'm grown up? If I did choose to go skinny-dipping with a man, it would be absolutely none of your business."

She missed Miguel's glower as she glanced again toward Devlin. Remembering how he looked all wet and glistening in the sun brought a new wave of heat to her cheeks. But she was resolute about not admitting embarrassment to her brother.

Zach laughed again and, holding his nose, sauntered over to pick up Dev's things. "What'll you give me for these pants, Wade?"

"You'll find out soon enough if you don't toss them here."

Miguel shouted out, "You got a beef with Mankiller, Major?"

"A beef?" Dev answered with surprise, catching the articles Zach tossed him. "Zach and I know each other from Washington. It was a shock seeing him out of his Brooks Brothers suit."

Zach remarked dryly, "This script is getting more interesting by the minute, Wade. I hope you don't mind if I stick around to see the end. Our old crowd might get a few chuckles out of this story at Marcia Winthrope's next cocktail party." His laughter took on a wicked dimension.

"You're loving every minute of this, aren't you, Mankiller?" Dev fought to still his chattering teeth as he shrugged into a wet shirt. He gave up trying to pull on soggy, wet pants in the deep lake. Buttoning several buttons on the shirt, he splashed into a shallow area. Having determined that his shirttails covered all the essentials, Dev stalked ashore, muttering to Zach as he passed, "*Et tu,* Brutus. Keep this up, old buddy, and we'll both go back to Washington in a pine box. Compliments of our friendly sheriff."

"Mike and I go way back," Zach whispered, spreading his palms. "But maybe not far enough...." He let a lazy smile skip over Miguel, pausing to linger on Pepper. "Where's he kept her hidden?"

Devlin didn't like the sudden gleam of interest that replaced the handsome attorney's smile, and he said so. "Quit salivating, Counselor, and get on back to your puberty rites. Try to remember you passed through yours two decades ago. This show is over." Raising his voice, he commanded Pepper, "You can leave now, too, Pepper. We'll handle it from here on—"

"Show's not quite over," interrupted Mike. "I'm still waiting for the truth." He stepped between Pepper and the two men before adding his command to Devlin's. "Wade did have one good idea, Sis. You get on back to the house. And put on something besides that damned nightshirt."

Even though he'd been the first to suggest it, Dev found that Miguel's high-handed manner rankled. "You've got the truth right under your nose, Rivera—or around your nose and in it."

Mike's gaze narrowed. Pepper threw up her hands and stormed up the trail. At the slope she turned. "Nobody appointed you my guardian protector, either, Devlin Wade. If there's anything I don't need, it's another overbearing brother. Mind your own business." Then covering her face with her hands, she left.

Dev yelled after her retreating form, "That might be one hell of a lot easier if it wasn't for you and that damned dog." Failing to gain a response, and losing the battle of not holding his nose, he reluctantly joined Zach and Mike.

A hawk circled lazily overhead, starkly outlined against a cornflower sky. Miguel measured Devlin for what seemed an eternity, then cleared his throat, addressing him in a tone that showed grudging respect.

"You don't lack gumption, Major. I like that. But standing up to a woman isn't the same as talkin' man to man. Suppose you tell *me* what you were doin' in the first place, out here in the buff—with my baby sister."

Devlin deliberately wrung water out of his soaking fatigues. The smile he gave Zach became icy as he turned to Mike. "I'm going to hang these out to dry. Then, Sheriff, I'm going to get dressed. After that, if you're still of a mind, we'll play twenty questions." Reaching out, he clasped Zach's hand. "It's always a pleasure, Counselor, but might I suggest a change in your after-shave before you go back to the big city?" He rubbed his nose. "A little too earthy—if you know what I mean." They both laughed. "But Zach, kidding aside, would you do me a favor? I'd like you to keep an ear to the ground around your old haunts. It's a gut feeling, but I'd like to know if sweet little Candy Huston is warming Major Bell's bed." Dev slung his pants over one arm. "I'll be at Fort Huachuca after next week."

Accepting Zach's nod as his word, Dev brushed past Miguel. On entering his camp, he heard the low rumble of Mike and Zach talking. But he trusted his old friend's discretion. Pepper's brother would have to work for whatever information he sought.

He was still smarting from Pepper's rebuke. He'd be damned if he could see a similarity between his honest caring and Miguel's overbearing attitude. That swipe she'd taken was uncalled for.

Dev dug out his last pair of clean fatigues. Well, maybe he *had* been playing protector. After all, he'd wanted to snatch her from under Zach's appraising eye. He'd trust Zach Mankiller with his life, but not with his woman. The way Zach collected damsels' hearts in D.C., he should more aptly have been named *lady*killer. But then, Dev thought sourly, Pepper wasn't his woman....

Thoughtfully Dev pulled on the heavy khaki pants. The day was already hot and again he cursed his East Coast gear. Shrugging into an olive-green undershirt, he dispensed with the regulation shirt and headed for the house.

Pepper had beaten him to the kitchen. Freshly scrubbed, she sat listening to Maria, both hands laced around an earthenware mug of coffee. As neither of the women noticed him, Dev stood silently for a moment in the doorway, studying Pepper. His heart didn't seem to be acting normally, and he fought a sudden weakness in his limbs.

She looked the same as she had yesterday and the day before—or did she? he asked himself. Yes. The bright copper strands of hair were still untamable and they still clashed outrageously with a vibrant fuchsia T-shirt, which was delicately molded to her shapely form in all the right places. But on closer inspection, Dev decided her face was a shade paler. Freckles he hadn't noticed yesterday formed a light pattern across the bridge of her nose, bringing out a certain innocence.

An uncommon urge to comfort her moved him to speak her name. "Pepper." It sounded harsher, more ragged, than he'd intended.

She glanced up, then just as quickly away. One hand slipped from her cup to caress a lazy yellow cat dozing in her lap.

Dev's mind took the picture and changed the setting to his Virginia farmhouse. The transition was altogether too smooth. Thrusting it away, he cleared his throat. "You're like the Pied Piper when it comes to collecting stray animals, aren't you?"

She frowned. "Don't cats like you, either, Major Wade?"

"I...I don't know." Devlin studied his shoes. "I've never had a cat. I've never owned any kind of animal. We were always moving, and I guess my mother never wanted the hassle of a pet." He frowned back.

"Maybe that explains some of your insensitivity," she muttered, gripping her cup tighter. Why did his simple admission play on her sympathy, blast him?

Maria held a cup out to Dev. "Coffee, Major? Hot and fresh—the only way to start a morning. Pepper was just telling me about the skunk. I'll bet Mike was livid. I think he figured you'd see Chief Broadhead's encampment and expected it to spook you." She laughed. "I love it when his jokes backfire."

Dev accepted the coffee, inhaling the aroma. So Miguel Rivera wanted to scare him off? How did that fit into the puzzle?

"Time I checked to see what's keeping Mike." Maria whisked off her apron and caught Dev's eye, indicating he should do something about Pepper's moody silence. "We've been invited over to the chief's for breakfast before the tourists hit." Her gaze became imploring. "Pepper's packed and ready to leave. Talk to her about staying, will you, Major?" From the doorway, Maria called, "We won't be gone long." The screen door banged on her heels.

Dev settled into the chair adjacent to Pepper's, tilted it back, and cradled his own cup between his palms. "Looks like Maria left us on our own for breakfast. If you haven't already eaten, I'll treat you to Omelette à-la-Wade. I know you think I'm completely helpless, but I'm not.''

Pepper swirled the coffee in her cup and gave an uncaring shrug. ''Fix whatever you want. I'm not hungry. You'll find pans in the cupboard next to the stove. I'm sure anything else you need will be in the fridge. I thought you didn't eat breakfast, Major.''

Dev studied her as she spoke. ''You promised me a scenic tour of a copper mine today. No self-respecting guide would undertake such a trip on an empty stomach.'' He tried a beguiling smile. It was a smile his own mother had never been able to resist.

Pepper glanced over at him and resisted. She ran her finger around and around the rim of her cup. ''Yesterday I had the impression you didn't think touring the mine could be considered entertainment,'' she said dully. ''Don't patronize me, Major Wade. Both you and Mike just embarrassed me, and in front of your friend, too. Isn't that humiliation enough?''

Dev's smile faded. The cat left Pepper, stretched, then leaped onto his lap. Absentmindedly, he stroked the soft fur.

''Suppose we talk about what's really bothering you, Pepper.'' He cut right to the heart of her agitation. ''Why don't you admit that *I* bother you. I don't fit your plan, whatever it is. Right?''

He got slowly to his feet, dropping the cat to the floor. He was fishing and he knew it. After washing and drying his hands, he rummaged in the pan cupboard until he found a skillet. The silence lengthened as he shuffled about the fridge, searching for eggs, cheese and fresh mushrooms.

''This isn't going to work,'' she said. ''Our traveling together to test the cot, I mean.''

The shuffling stopped. Dev backed out of the refrigerator with hands filled and overflowing. He took in the flush of Pepper's cheeks and the taut set of her jaw before he nudged the door closed with one knee, depositing his finds on the counter.

"Oh?" Expertly he cracked six eggs into a bowl. "I thought we were getting the hang of things. You did notice I set up the cots and the tents last night. What's not working?"

Pepper slid from the chair, crossed the tile floor and dumped cold coffee down the drain. Careful not to look at Dev or touch him, she picked up the pot from the stove and refilled her cup.

"You didn't really ask to be here—" she began.

Dev cut her off. "No—but you didn't object much when my father gave the order." He melted butter in the hot pan, then poured in the frothy egg mixture. "What's changed? I just want to be certain that selling the cot is the only reason for this trip."

"Of course it is." Pepper stepped back and leaned against the sink. "Or at least it was." Frowning, she sipped her coffee. She didn't like the way she was beginning to feel when she was near Devlin Wade. And she didn't like wondering what it would be like to kiss him again. More to the point, perhaps, she didn't like him ordering her around. "I don't think a cryptologist is the right man for the job," she said defensively.

Devlin folded in the sliced mushrooms, then quickly grated cheese over the top. "I had the misfortune to be going in your direction. I imagine there's someone you'd rather have along." Reminded suddenly of General Huston's devious wife, Dev's stomach tightened.

"You mean someone in the army? Hardly," she scoffed. "I suppose I should be grateful that you aren't using this— and me—to make points with my father like some officers might." Her lips were set and her eyes steely.

Dev hit the lever on the toaster and watched the bread disappear. So, the Red Hot Pepper had a man, an officer, in her past. But at the moment, that was the least of his concerns. Deliberately Dev changed the subject. "Why did you come to my defense down at the lake if I'm so disreputable?"

Pepper whirled on him. Coffee sloshed over the rim of the cup.

"I heard Smedley barking. With his track record, I figured he'd treed another cat." A half smile twitched the corners of her lips. "Little did I know it was a civet cat—that's another name for skunk." She shrugged, letting go of the smile. "It was a shock seeing you, Major. Seeing you...well, you know..." She blushed, looking away. "I stayed because I didn't like what Mike was insinuating about us—about you. I should have known you'd be just as dictatorial as he is. Obviously my concern for your welfare was misplaced."

Devlin snatched the pan from the stove. He'd almost burned the omelette. He cut it in two, then placed the halves on two plates, which he put on opposite sides of the table. Gruffly he motioned her to eat. Since those moments at the lake, when he'd held her in his arms, he'd been remembering what it was like to kiss her. He wondered if she always tasted of cinnamon and orange spice. But damn it all, they'd both be better off if he changed the subject and stopped wondering so much. "If you feel that way, I'm surprised you didn't throw me to the wolves—or in this case, your brother," he drawled sarcastically. "I didn't know you cared."

His voice sent shivers of apprehension up her spine. Pepper pushed her plate aside and jumped up with her cup on the pretense of filling it. "Don't read something that isn't there, Major. I would have done the same for Pete or Mike or for any of my brothers."

In an instant, Devlin was behind her, spinning her around.

Surprised, Pepper dropped the cup on the counter with a crash.

"We aren't brother and sister." His voice trembled, as did his whispery breath fanning her cheek. Catching her by the shoulders, he pulled her roughly against him.

She could feel the rise and fall of his chest. Closing her eyes, Pepper held her breath, lest her pulse leap to match his.

"Open your eyes. Look at me," he demanded harshly. "I'm not your brother. Nor am I some nameless officer you've got a grudge against." He paused until her eyes flew open. "Not family, not Major—just a man, one Devlin Wade." Ruthlessly he inched her closer until his lips were on hers.

Pepper shut her eyes again and let him take his kiss, determined to resist, until unknowingly she gave back. In confusion, her mind battled with her senses. She'd lied about having sisterly feelings, and it was difficult to remember why she didn't like officers—this officer—as her hands followed the ropy muscles of Dev's forearms upward to loop around his neck.

He'd unleashed more passion than he'd intended, Dev thought as his fingers inched her knit top from the waistband of her shorts. When his hands made contact with the warm skin on her back, he groaned low in his throat, pressed tighter to her gentle curves and let the kiss deepen naturally, matching her tremble for tremble.

In the lucid part of his brain, he experienced a powerful relaxing of his restless soul. But there were so many reasons he needed to go slow, he told himself. There was his father's manipulating him into this trip. There was his resignation and the antagonism of Pepper's brother. But none of those things really mattered, he argued, letting Pepper's shirt creep higher, and he took pleasure from his hands molding lazy patterns across her back.

Pepper struggled to remember why she shouldn't be kissing him. Clear thinking evaporated like smoke escaping through a chimney. She touched his hair, his cheek, his chest, wanting only to savor more. That long-ago dream of independence seemed unimportant now.

Tasting, nibbling on Pepper's full lower lip, Dev almost missed the sound of a heavy tread on the porch. The slam of a screen door brought his submerged senses to half-alert.

Still he was slow to end the all-consuming kiss and pull away.

"You two finished with breakfast?"

Miguel Rivera braced one hand against the refrigerator and leaned into it. His other sun-browned hand rested loosely above a low-riding gun.

Pepper stared blankly at her brother, then blinked rapidly, emerging as though from a thick fog. Dazedly she backed away from Devlin.

Maria squeezed past her husband's imposing frame, grinned at Dev and reached for the coffeepot. "Too hot this morning to eat anyhow. The day's gonna be a scorcher."

"Uh-huh," Devlin answered her, using the brief respite to slow his pulse. He let his hand trail possessively down Pepper's back, not really caring that Mike had caught him kissing her.

He reached for the cup Maria offered, his hand shaking. She steadied his hand, with a look of gentle understanding. When she glanced covertly at her husband, Devlin realized Maria thought he was afraid of Mike. He wasn't. Pepper, wearing those damned lavender shorts and fuchsia top, was the greater threat.

Still, Dev couldn't dispute the sheriff's impressive impact, especially dressed as he was, head to toe in black. Shirt, pants, snakeskin boots, the continuity broken only by a glittering silver star on the left pocket of his shirt—that, too, was impressive. Yesterday, Dev might have given ground to Miguel's tough exterior. Today, feeling that Pepper had wormed a tiny toehold in his life—or was it the other way around?—he gave the man no quarter.

"You still looking to have that talk, Sheriff?" Dev raised his cup and slanted his head toward the oak table in bold invitation.

Seething at her own capitulation and at their easy dismissal of her presence, Pepper snatched up her plate and turned away. She would rather her brother hadn't walked in on them, but she wouldn't defend her actions to him. "It's time I got my gear together."

"Don't run off, Sis. Mankiller's gonna bring your dog back as soon as he gets the tomato juice washed out and I wanna see if I got the air in your car fixed." Miguel's large frame blocked Pepper's exit.

Maria shifted her position. Stepping around her, Miguel clapped Dev on the shoulder. "When Pop called, saying he and your old man set things up and we were supposed to roll out the red carpet for you, I'll admit I wasn't pleased. Ruben and I handpicked a rancher over in Larkspur for our little sis."

Mike yanked open the refrigerator and pulled out two beers. Before he could offer Dev one, Maria glided between them and snatched both cans from her husband's grasp. "You're on duty." Raising one delicate eyebrow, she pointed to the door. "Pepper and Major Wade have things to do besides listen to you spin yarns about what you and Ruben cook up when you go out painting the town red." She nudged him.

"All right, woman," he grumbled. "If you'll take my advice, Wade, you won't let those romantic old fools hustle you to the altar. If even half of Mankiller's stories are true, son of a gun, you guys have the best of both worlds. A wife does have a way of clipping your wings." Smiling, he bent to kiss Maria's cheek, taking the sting from his words, as she shooed him toward the door.

"Wait!" Pepper's directive halted Mike's lazy progress.

"Repeat what you just said, Mike. Pop told you what?" She turned to face her brother squarely, defiance returning fire to her eyes. Her hands rested on her hips in anger.

Mike shot Maria a warning glance. Dev recognized it for what it was because he stood in direct line of the look that passed between them. Like magic, another piece of his puzzle fell into place. Not one but two manipulative fathers were at work in this matchmaking. That little tidbit of information changed the whole picture. It would be interesting to see what Pepper had to say about this turn of events.

"Are you suggesting General Wade sent Devlin on this mission for a reason other than to test my cot for the army?'' Her tone remained stubborn, disbelieving. Her stance challenged Miguel.

The sheriff shook his head and laughed. ''Frankly, I wondered what was wrong with General Wade's son that he couldn't find a wife on his own.'' He paused to give Dev a knowing wink. ''According to Mankiller, the man has legions of ladies standing in line. Simmer down, Sis, Pop's done okay this time. You'd better not run this one off.''

Pepper's growl of outrage, complete with tightly balled fists, told Devlin she'd been oblivious to the plan. Thinking only to defuse the situation, he stepped between brother and sister, stating calmly, ''I know my father likes to map out my life, Rivera. For him it's as natural as breathing. What I find hard to believe is that any of you feel your sister is incapable of attracting a man on her own.''

As Pepper sputtered, Mike laughed louder.

''We spent the first eighteen years keeping her in a protective shell. Then she popped out, and we've spent the last seven years trying to stuff her in again.'' He punched Dev's shoulder companionably, making him wince. ''Surely you've noticed her evil temper by now. The chili Pepper has not been an easy sell.'' A second wink was cut short as all his energy was consumed holding off her attack.

''Hey, Sis! I was only kidding, okay? Rube and I do our best to keep Pop happy by obliging his little idiosyncrasies. He thinks you need a husband.'' Miguel made a dash for the door with Pepper hot on his heels.

Maria turned pleading eyes on Devlin, shrugging her slender shoulders helplessly before offering an explanation. ''Five older brothers and a general for a father... it is difficult for a motherless girl. Maybe Pepper doesn't like military men, but this rancher in Larkspur isn't right for her. She will be very angry over Ruben's and Mike's latest interference.''

Dev could hear Pepper's angry voice and Miguel's deeper one. He thought about the way she'd responded to his kiss. Shaking his head, he said to Maria, ''Right now, she must be feeling a little like the all-or-nothing stakes in a crap game, and she's already told me once today to mind my own business. I don't relish being told twice.''

Maria arched a brow.

Dev recalled the spicy promise of Pepper's kiss. He weighed it against the empty vacuum his life had become. Telling himself his decision had everything to do with Maria's accusing look, he strode through the door and into the heat of a sibling argument.

It wasn't that he was throwing down the gauntlet, he told himself; he was intervening because Maria expected it. And yet, there was a certain satisfaction in the thought that just maybe Gentleman Win and the Rivera clan would find they'd met their match in Devlin Wade.

CHAPTER SEVEN

   Rrring.

"Hallo! You've got the judge. State your business.

"Oh, it's you Miguel. Yeah, Pop called. What a lame-brain scheme.

"Just because you met the dude and made a snap judgment doesn't mean Pepper should marry him. You know I've got this rancher, Ken Boyd, in mind. Raises horses—has a firm hand with the fillies.

"Okay, okay, I'll check this Wade character out. Maybe!"

   Slam. Click.

"OF ALL THE NO-GOOD, sneaky, conniving things to do," Pepper sputtered as she neatly angled the Ferrari into a curbside parking space. She voiced her annoyance at both generals, Wade and Rivera, without so much as taking a breath between one picturesque phrase and the next.

Listening patiently, Dev ignored her railing, as he'd done the entire way between Burro Peak and Larkspur. He leaned forward and adjusted his sunglasses, then gazed out the windshield, scanning both sides of a narrow street lined with weathered adobe buildings. "I don't know why we're stopping," he remarked, placing a hand over his heart, "but I can tell you this, it's none too soon. I've listened to your repertoire of derogatory adjectives two times through. My ears could use a rest." A teasing grin creased his face, and in the same light vein, he ran a finger lightly down her cheek and over her grimly set lips.

Pepper slapped his hand away. Her face softened only a little with his touch. "You could have thrown in your six-bits' worth any time, Major Wade. I'm sure your West Point vocabulary would put mine to shame." Her lips resumed their tight line. "It makes me mad all over again to think they presumed to arrange my life. Our lives!" she corrected. Then she flushed. "I don't know how you can be so blasé. But then, you military types *like* taking orders."

Devlin studied her a moment, wondering what she would say if he told her he disliked orders enough to quit taking them altogether. No, he decided quickly. After all, she was still a general's daughter. What he said instead was, "Neither your father nor mine are available for hanging and all your steam is wasted on me. Besides, we agree in theory." He tried to look serious, but his lips curled in a smile. "Don't you think it's time you called me plain Devlin and forgot I've been to West Point? I don't happen to agree that my vocabulary is broader than yours. I can't think of many insults you missed. But what we might be able to agree on is that not one of your brothers is worth a damn as a mechanic. This air conditioner still isn't working."

Devlin peeled off his sunglasses and squinted toward the intersection. "Hey, not to change the subject, but where are we, anyhow? I thought your brother Ruben owned a ranch."

Pepper's careless wave encompassed the block of squat buildings set back from the sidewalk on the far side of the street.

"Welcome to Larkspur. Ruben's ranch is a few miles to the west. That's the courthouse you see over there." Pepper plucked a folded piece of paper from the dash and waved it in Dev's face. "If you remember, I have a speeding ticket to pay. Courtesy of the patrolman you were so chummy with out on the back road. This transaction shouldn't take me long," she added brightly.

Holding the ticket firmly in one hand, Pepper cracked the door ajar. She could see no reason to tell Dev that the lone magistrate in Larkspur was her brother. She wanted Ruben all to herself for the time being. If anyone could tell her what Pop was really up to, it would be Ruben. "Stay," she commanded Smedley sharply when the dog tried to follow. "No more skunks for you."

"For a minute there, I thought you meant me." Sliding out the passenger door, Dev gave a teasing wink, punctuating his words with a lazy yawn and a languid stretch.

Pepper stared at him. Her knees grew weak and a tingle ran lightly over her arms and up her neck. Before she found the strength to answer, a group of rowdy teenage boys, horsing around with each other as they wandered down the walkway, drew abreast of the Ferrari and eyed the gleaming red car appreciatively, expressing as much in fluid Spanish.

Pepper stepped to the sidewalk near the hood. Immediately the young men transferred their attention to her bright shorts. They murmured more loudly, punched each other playfully and made cow eyes. One clutched his chest over his heart, pretending to be smitten.

Dev knew the boys were teasing. Though he didn't understand a word of their soft-spoken tongue, he had no difficulty understanding their meaning. They spoke a universal language shared by all young men, young or old, when it came to admiring fast cars and beautiful women. But when it came to Pepper, he found he didn't like it.

Staking his claim nonverbally, Dev shot them a challenging look. Amid much laughter and mocking salutes in deference to his uniform, the little group ambled on down the street. Their final thumbs-up signal paid homage to Dev's possession of the Ferrari and the woman. His body language was universal, too. He'd moved in close beside her and wrapped an arm around her waist.

Pepper felt her cheeks grow crimson. Spanish was her second language and she'd understood every word of their fast exchange. However, it was Devlin's arm at her waist that somehow seemed more threatening than the group of teens. Just as she opened her mouth to object, he cut in.

"You can't go into the courthouse dressed like that." His frown deepened as he examined her brief attire.

Distracted, Pepper paused to check her clean T-shirt and new shorts appraisingly. She raised one eyebrow.

"Why not?"

"It's too...too...little material." Dev's open palm indicated the brevity of her shorts. Seeing hostility flash deep within her cat-green eyes, he dropped his hand from her waist and stepped away.

Facing him squarely, Pepper recognized his combative hands-on-hips stance and immediately bristled, though strangely, she missed his proprietary touch.

"Why don't you climb back in the car and take a nice siesta with the dog, Major? As I started to say earlier at Mike's, I already have a few too many overbearing males in my life thinking they can order me around. I sure don't need another." Turning on one heel, she boldly jaywalked across the street.

"Dammit, Pepper—wait!" Sidestepping to avoid a chugging old pickup, Dev jogged after her. He caught up with her on the sidewalk and clamped his right hand around her upper arm.

She tugged ineffectually against his fingers. But deep down, she really didn't try hard. Something about Devlin Wade once again seemed inconsistent with what she knew of officers—or thought she did. Not trusting how she felt, Pepper reverted to sarcasm.

"You can't seem to resist giving orders, can you? Don't try to mold me into one of your obedient little sheep, Major. I'm sorry your father ordered you to come." Suddenly her tone shifted and the angry set of her jaw softened. "I really do understand how you feel about not having any choice in the matter." She sighed. "It happens to me a lot. You know, we can go straight to the base instead of Ruben's ranch when we leave here. We don't have to camp out to please your father."

Pepper continued quietly. "The man who manufactures my inventions said we could probably market my cot to a recreational-equipment firm. Or I could sell the Ferrari and move out from under my father's roof. Just don't you start on me, too. I think I have more relatives planning my life than you do yours, and mine have had more practice. Besides, you take orders by choice. With me, it's happenstance." Using her other hand, Pepper pried Dev's fingers loose.

His heart labored, sounding an alarm. Dev already knew he wanted a chance to explore what he was beginning to feel for her. But he couldn't honestly think of a single valid reason for suggesting they continue the trip, if she chose to end it here. Listening to her now, he suddenly realized he knew so little about Mary Kate Rivera, the woman. She probably knew much more about him—the army grapevine was good for that.

What they needed, and the thought jolted him, was time alone for comparing lives and sharing truths. Time for caring, loving and maybe, just maybe, growing old together. The urge to tell her was so overpowering it had him backing off. Slowly he eased the curl of his fingers.

"We'll discuss this later, Pepper. It's nothing to be decided in the middle of the street. Go on ahead and pay your fine." His tone softened to match hers. "I saw a small department store in the block we just passed. I think I'll go see what they have in cooler menswear. These heavy khakis are out of place in this heat." He glanced down at the stiff, wrinkled fatigues. "And just for the record," he said, rubbing the sleeve of her T-shirt between thumb and forefinger, "in every flock there's always a black sheep—and it manages to survive, obedient or not."

A grin twitched at the corners of Pepper's mouth. Major Wade was human after all. What surprised her was that he hadn't jumped at the chance to dump her project. Because he was so obviously trying, she teased him back.

"I hope you don't expect Ralph Lauren or Izod in Estebar's," she joked, showing him a full smile. "You won't be G.Q. when you come out, but if you buy cotton shirts and shorts, I guarantee you'll be a lot cooler for the remainder of the trip.''

"So I'll be a cool sheep in wolf's clothing after visiting Estebar's." Keeping a straight face, Dev gave one final tug on her sleeve, letting it snap back, before he spun on his heel and trotted off toward the store. He was midway down the block when he turned to look at her again. His chuckle broke into a belly laugh. Lord, but it felt good to release the tension she created in him. His nerves had been stretched tight since the very first hour they'd met. It was time he admitted, at least to himself, that he found her beautiful, capable and feisty, possessing both strength and softness. And what did she see when she looked at him? he wondered.

Slowing to a walk, Dev stuck his hands in his pockets. His exuberance dimmed. He wished there was more time for him and Pepper to explore some of the more important issues between them before they arrived at brother Ruben's. Especially before Ruben trotted out his handpicked wealthy rancher.

Stealing another quick look, Dev grunted his satisfaction. Pepper was still standing where he'd left her, the speeding ticket clutched tightly to her breast. She seemed to be devouring him with her eyes. Facing west again, Dev whistled a lighthearted tune as he pushed open the glass door to Estebar's. He broke off abruptly. Was he really going to let Gentleman Win get away with this? The thought was sobering.

BECAUSE SHE'D LEFT her sunglasses in the Ferrari, Pepper had to narrow her eyes against the afternoon sun as her gaze followed Dev's shadowy outline. Only when he disappeared into the clothing store did she release the breath she'd been holding since his parting comment. She tried not caring what prompted him to make it and found she cared too much.

She was annoyed that he had the power to leave her speechless. Annoyed that her pulse quickened as she watched him walk—no, saunter was a better term for his lazy, easy gait. "Blast," she muttered, turning toward the courthouse. What was there about this particular man—this particular officer, she reminded herself grimly—that exacted such a primitive response from her? Whatever it was, it came close to overshadowing the need to declare her independence.

Frustrated because she had no ready answer, Pepper expended her pent-up energy opening the heavy door. The cool tiled entry of the old adobe building sent a shiver up her spine. Or was it caused by a sudden intrusive memory of that kiss in Mike's kitchen? Something urged her to run after Devlin Wade. Logic made her stay.

"What do you need? It's siesta time." A reedy voice assaulted Pepper from behind a desk in a shadowy alcove.

She stepped closer to the desk, examining the bright black eyes staring at her from a lined and weathered face.

"I'm here to see Judge Rivera," Pepper announced, waving the ticket before the assessing eyes.

"Come back at three. Someone will take the money for your fine. Judge doesn't need to see you for a simple ticket." Dismissively the old woman behind the desk pulled a serape around her shoulders, tilted back in her chair and closed her eyes.

Pepper bit her lip and gazed down the empty corridor. It had been several years since she'd visited Ruben at the courthouse. She couldn't remember which of the closed doors led to his office. Somewhere in the distance, she imagined she heard the squeak of hinges and the grate of metal, a quixotic reminder that this scarred old building housed the county jail. She glanced down at the gooseflesh on her legs and was troubled to think Dev had been right about the inappropriateness of her dress.

"Ruben is my brother," Pepper blurted out, jumping with a start when the old woman's chair crashed against the floor.

"Sure he is, lady. And I'm the Queen Mother." The woman slapped her knee and cackled. Abruptly she stopped

laughing, and the black eyes scanned Pepper from head to
toe and back again. "Judge Rivera is as Mexican as I am,
child. Now, I don't know whose idea of a joke this is, but
the good judge don't mess with the likes of you. You run
along. He's got a nice Mexican wife."

Pepper's green eyes glittered indignantly. Tossing back
her heavy mane of red hair, she approached the desk and
slapped the ticket down. Through clenched teeth and in
fluent Spanish, she challenged, "Mary Kathleen Angelina
Rivera, daughter of General Raul Rivera. Where did you say
I could find Ruben?" After learning of her father's chica-
nery from Mike, she didn't feel this was a day to be calling
on family ties.

The woman's jaw went slack as she stared down at the
scribbled ticket. She stammered, "The regular receptionist
had an errand to run during siesta and asked me to take her
place. She told me not to let anyone in until three o'clock.
I'm only doing what I was told. You can't blame me. You
don't look like a Rivera."

Pepper grimaced. How many times had she heard that
statement? Maybe that was why the family was so possessive. To make her feel like she belonged. "Where is Rub-
en's office?" The question sounded far more brittle than
she'd intended.

"He's downstairs catchin' a nap in one of the empty
cells." The dark head tilted toward the door marked Stairs.
"You better be tellin' me the truth, you hear?" The raspy
reproach floated after Pepper and echoed down the stair-
well along with her staccato footsteps. There was no sense
venting her anger on the woman behind the desk. Perhaps
what hurt so much was that suddenly it seemed as if the
whole family was trying to palm her off on some man—any
man. It didn't help to know that the only man to whom she
might give a second thought had reluctantly been thrust into
the same situation by his own father.

"Ruben," Pepper called hesitantly into a dim room. She
paused near an open door as she saw his broad frame
stretched the length of a sagging cot at the back of a cell.

Automatically her lips formed a smile and the ice melted from around her heart. She loved this brother most of all, this patient man who always had time for a tagalong little sister. A man who understood that a teenage girl's tough facade was often just that, all veneer. She knew Ruben would listen to her woes concerning Major Wade. He would comfort, then advise. She wouldn't believe what Miguel had claimed about Papa until she heard it from Ruben, though he, too, was a Rivera through and through. Pepper's voice was soft and slightly wistful. "Come on sleepyhead, wake up. Siesta is over. What would Larkspur's finest say if they knew their esteemed judge was hiding out in a cell like a common criminal?"

The man on the cot stirred, sat up and winced to avoid the light. He reached for a heavy black robe loosely draped across a straight-backed chair and shrugged into it. Stifling a yawn, he stared at the woman standing in the doorway with arms crossed.

"Pepper," he exclaimed, raking a hand through thick black hair, leaving it askew, all peaks and valleys. "It's really you? I was ready to wring Chiquita's neck. What the hell are you doing here, scaring me out of my wits?" He frowned up at her. "Pop said . . ." Ruben paused and raked a hand through his hair again. "Well, never mind what Pop said." He flushed guiltily. "Come here and let me look at you." Standing, he reached out both arms. The hem of his black robe fell to the floor, making him look every inch the imposing judge.

Pepper rushed into his open arms. His bear hug left her breathless. "Oh, Ruben. It's so good to see you. Don't blame Chiquita for my interrupting your sleep. It was someone else, an older woman, one about Grandmother Rivera's age. And she didn't want to let me see you. In fact, dressed as I am, she suspected my motives for being here. I wouldn't be a bit surprised if that's her I hear clomping down the stairs right now, coming to check out my story." Pepper smiled up at him. "When did you talk to Pop? Just wait until you hear what he's up to this time."

"Pepper?" The shocked query issued from the doorway was not from the old woman. It was Devlin Wade's husky voice, carrying a note of disapproval that had Pepper twisting sharply in Ruben's arms.

"Friend of yours, honey?" Ruben let his arms fall from around Pepper's waist. "This place hasn't seen so much traffic since the last roundup," he murmured in her ear, not taking his eyes from the tense man framed in the opening.

Pepper stared at Dev, her eyes widening as she drank in the sight of him. Slowly her arms slid from Ruben's neck, though she still leaned against him for support.

Dev had indeed bought new clothes. Soft white shorts proved a perfect foil for his tanned, well-muscled legs. A navy blue tank top sharply defined the muscles of his arms and chest. A thicket of dark chest hair curled invitingly from the ribbing around the low neckline. New white tennis shoes on sockless feet completed his outfit and added to the over-all masculine effect.

Pepper breathed deeply, willing her knees to keep her upright. Damn, but the man was close to her idea of perfection. She was stunned to discover she didn't want their relationship, however fragile, however unsuitable, to end. But she was too caught up in her own distress to register the shock radiating from Dev's cold blue eyes.

"Just what is the fee for speeding in this county, pray tell?" The icy sarcasm of Dev's question matched the murderous gleam in his eye.

Ruben studied his sister. "Speeding? What's this about speeding? I knew you'd get into trouble with that flashy race car."

Pepper shrank from the sparks that shot at her from Devlin's accusing eyes. Wordlessly she handed Ruben the crumpled ticket. He stepped away long enough to smooth it out, then held it at arm's length to see more clearly.

"So, Preston Carlyle is riding herd over in the wilderness rim area, huh? Tell me he didn't know you were my sister. I already owe that joker two six-packs of Corona, because Mike was in such a hurry to get home from our last poker party he used half a brain and a lead foot. What did the young scoundrel demand this time? My blood?'' Ruben pushed Pepper down on the cot he'd just vacated and waved the speeding ticket in front of her nose, seeming to forget Dev Wade existed.

Jealousy and shock turned to amusement when Devlin tumbled to the fact that he'd been duped for a second time by one of Pepper's hulking brothers. His laughter bubbled up, drawing Ruben's censure.

The older man loosed an oath in Spanish. Pepper scrambled off the cot to stand beside her brother. "Ruben, calm down. Carlyle didn't know we were related, though I can tell you I was tempted to bring it up. Major Wade—'' she tipped her head toward Devlin ''—nearly convinced him I was a gun moll for a team of bank robbers who knocked off a bank in Elephant Butte. You should be thankful you don't have to rescue me from his pokey.'' Glancing back, she was relieved to find Dev, one shoulder lodged against the door frame, looking relaxed, and smiling.

"So you're Pop's jack-a-dandy? I surmised as much,'' stated Ruben, leaving the cell and thrusting a beefy hand toward Dev.

Devlin backed away, holding up one palm. "I hope you don't mind if we simply say hello, Rivera. Your brother Miguel tried to grind my fingers into dust when we met. Frankly I can do without another lesson in bone crushing. And I don't consider myself a jack-a-dandy.''

Ruben laughed heartily, slapping Dev on the back. "Hey, you're all right, Wade. Come on up to my office and we'll talk a little about my pop, your pop, and Mike. Frankly, this entire convoluted story sounds interesting to me. If my afternoon docket cancels, we'll go next door to Angel's Tavern and bend our elbows a bit. Best way to judge a man, I've found. Come on.'' He hustled Dev out the door.

"Hey,'' shouted Pepper, "what about me?'' Two guilty faces appeared back in the doorway. Looking chagrined, both men motioned Pepper to follow. Suddenly reluctant, she dragged her feet. It bothered her to find she was jealous of their easy camaraderie. Ruben was *her* brother. He should be listening to her side of the story, not Devlin Wade's.

She trudged slowly behind them up the stairs. The men were deep in conversation when she arrived at Ruben's office, and they hadn't seemed to miss her. They were discussing West Point and the Pentagon. Two subjects Pepper found distasteful.

"If you two are going to swap fish stories, then I'm going on out to the ranch. Ruben, you won't mind giving Major Wade a ride, will you?" Her tone was just short of churlish. "By the way," she added, as she reached the door, "since you both found my speeding ticket so amusing, maybe one of you can take care of paying it. If you need me for anything," she said with saccharine sweetness, "Smedley and I will be with Elena."

Pepper heard Dev asking about Elena, and Ruben grilling him in turn about Smedley, as she slammed the door. She loitered outside for a few moments, not consciously expecting Devlin to follow her, yet not believing for a minute he'd actually stay. Slowly, very slowly, she crossed to the Ferrari. Though the car was on the shady side of the street and Dev had left the window cracked for Smedley, the inside of the car was stifling.

She let Smedley out, filled his water bowl from a Thermos and delayed leaving. Finally it looked as if Devlin really intended to stay behind. And because she could stall no longer, Pepper flicked the Ferrari to life, pausing only to slide the sunroof open a breathing space. That small act claimed her attention long enough for her to miss Dev's marathon dash across a suddenly congested street.

Her surprise was genuine when he rapped sharply on her window. Automatically her foot hit the brake, and she wasn't aware of following the play of his muscles as he rounded the hood, until he reminded her impatiently that the passenger door was locked. Pepper was glad he couldn't see how unsteady her hand was as she unlatched the door.

Settling into the seat, Dev snapped on his seat belt before allowing Smedley to lick his fingers. Without taking his eyes from Pepper's, he smoothed the dog's ears with his other hand. "You owe me fifty dollars, lady," he charged lightly. "Your fine was forty-five. I threw a fifty-dollar bill at Ruben when I realized you actually intended leaving without me. I told him to buy Carlyle's beer with the tip. You and I, however, will negotiate for the entire fifty."

"I'll give it to you as soon as we get to the ranch. I don't like owing anyone." Pepper whipped the car into a tight U-turn and headed west. A tiny smile accompanied her promise.

"Good Lord! A U-turn in front of the courthouse. Are you nuts? Of course you are," Devlin said, answering his own question. "But that's beside the point, and to get back to what you were saying, did you mean you especially don't like owing *me*?"

"What makes you think I'd dislike owing you over anyone else?" she asked, slowing the car while she checked in the rearview mirror.

"Well, we never settled the issue of what it is about me that gets your hackles up. Suppose you tell me. Back there, you seemed more than willing to let Ruben give me the third degree—good ole boy style, in a smoky bar with plenty of tongue-loosening beer."

Pepper looked perplexed. "Yes, that would be Ruben's style. He huffs and puffs a lot, but of all my brothers, he's the one who usually takes time to hear me out."

"So is your nose out of joint because you thought he might listen to me?"

"Maybe something like that crossed my mind," she admitted stiffly. The air inside the car suddenly seemed excessively warm. Pepper didn't like the way their discussion was headed. In spite of what Mike had said about Ruben's having a rancher he wanted her to meet, she had intended to seek her older brother's advice in dealing with some of the emotions Devlin Wade stirred in her. Pepper looked on

Ruben as *her* confidant, and she really hadn't wanted him to hear Devlin's view of the situation first.

"I get the distinct feeling your old man has systematically gone about trying to enlist your brothers' support in throwing us together. I'm also getting the message that Mike and Ruben have been through this before. Do you have other brothers conveniently stashed along this trek?" Dev removed his sunglasses to get a clearer look at her.

"You aren't likely to meet my other two brothers," Pepper stated shortly. "You'll meet Papa when you check in at Fort Huachuca. Be prepared for a steamroller, too. When Papa gets his mind set on something, there's no stopping him." Her tone was glum. "Hey...I really am sorry you've been railroaded into this."

Pepper had reached the outskirts of the quiet town and now she speeded up. A rush of wind lifted the heavy hair from around her face and blew curling strands willy-nilly out the open window and through the sunroof. Dev stared raptly. It was the way he remembered seeing her that very first time from the staff car.

The lady in the red dress had fascinated him then, and this vibrant woman sitting by his side still did. He wound a strand of hair—more gold than red—around his finger, enjoying the silken texture. He'd dreamed last night of seeing it spread across his pillow, tangled and tasting of sultry cinnamon oil laced with tangy orange spice.

"It isn't your fault my father and yours think alike," he admitted grudgingly to keep himself from thinking about last night's dream. "Must be Bully 101, a class they have to take before they make General. I guess what would serve both of them right is for us to somehow turn the tables," he murmured absently. The corners of his lips tilted upward in a wry smile, and he tugged playfully at the red-gold curl he'd captured. "Maybe we could each announce plans to marry someone they can't tolerate." Devlin carefully turned her chin toward him until their eyes met. "Do you have someone in your life who fits that description?" It was the first time he'd actually thought to consider whether or not she had a boyfriend. Someone maybe her family didn't like. Someone, he knew right now, he wouldn't like.

"That's it!" Pepper whipped the steering wheel sharply to the right causing them to bump off the asphalt onto a sandy layby. Once off the road, she brought the Ferrari to a skidding halt. Sand rolled over the gleaming car in engulfing waves, choking them as it blew in their open side windows.

Dev coughed and shook loose the curl he'd been holding. Smedley sneezed on them from the small area behind their heads. Incredulous, Dev looked at her. "What's up now? Don't you ever do anything in half measures, Pepper?" He rubbed the grit from his eyes. "Of course you don't," he said, answering his own question once again. "Why would I even suggest it?"

She couldn't contain her excitement. It radiated from her eyes and lit her face with an impish smile. "You and I," she bubbled delightedly. "We could turn the tables on those old codgers. Try to imagine what two old-fashioned generals would deem a fate worse than death for their precious offspring."

Dev shook his head slowly. "You and I being their precious offspring, right? Why is it that already I don't think I'm going to like whatever devious little plan you're cooking up? But let's have it straight from the hip, before I discard it."

"My father would explode if I decided to *live* with some man instead of marrying him." Pepper's smile erupted into a full-blown victorious chuckle. "After meeting your father, I would bet my last dollar he feels the same way." Her grin turned smug.

Dev simply stared at her, waiting for more of the plan to unfold. She stared back, smiling a Cheshire-cat smile. At last, Dev's brows knotted into a frown. "What are you proposing? That you...that we...?" He shook his head warily. "Let me get this straight. You, the self-proclaimed hater of all things military, officers in particular, are suddenly proposing to set up housekeeping with me, a major, at a base where your father is in command?''

Pepper's smile vanished. "Well, not exactly." She shifted in her seat, looking everywhere but at him. Her face flamed. What made the suggestion sound so tawdry when he laid it out like that? she wondered.

"What, then?" he demanded, snapping the fingers of one hand, ordering Smedley to sit. Then just as swiftly, he wrapped both of his hands around Pepper's upper arms and yanked her out of her seat until she looked him in the eye. Their noses nearly touched.

"More like...pretend?" The question was hesitant. Soft and breathless, because she wanted to escape the penetrating blue of his eyes. Her own grew darkly troubled as she shied from the anger that seemed to instantly harden his gaze.

Dev was first to draw away. "Pretend, Pepper?" he questioned in a rough-edged growl. "I think not. You're too much a woman and I'm too much a man for us to play little-girl-and-boy games." Pushing her harshly away, he grabbed for his sunglasses and hid behind their mirrored lenses. Disappointment, pain—both ripped through his chest. He thought of the hurt it would bring his mother, of the way Pepper's traditional family would feel. Hell, it was the way he felt, too. "Your father and my father are not only generals but role models for every man who signs on under them. You want to strike back at them, Pepper, but it all goes a lot deeper, has a lot more impact than you seem to understand." He closed his eyes and passed a hand over the tight line of his jaw. He needed a shave, he thought irrelevantly.

Smedley butted him with his shaggy head and whined. Dev shrugged him away and turned to stare at the empty miles of endless, barren wasteland. Disappointment hurt far worse than distrust, he decided.

Pepper battled a hard knot that was forming in her stomach as she traced the curve of the steering wheel with a trembling finger. Devlin Wade didn't want her. He didn't even want to pretend to want her. What had she tasted in a few meaningless kisses that ever made her think he might be different from other military men? But he *was* different. What he had said to her meant that Major Wade did, at least, have principles. She was the one who should be embarrassed by her behavior.

"We'll just forget it," she mumbled, chewing harder on her lip. If only she thought before she blurted right out with things—but that had been a downfall she'd battled, it seemed, forever. "I'll think of something else. Something less humiliating for both of us, Major." Then to cover her shame, Pepper buried her face in Smedley's soft fur.

"Well, you'd better think fast. Your brother, the judge, just drove by and now he's backing up. From the looks of him, I'd say he's already tried us for some indiscretion and now he's ready for the hanging."

CHAPTER EIGHT

WEDNESDAY, LARKSPUR, New Mexico
  Rrring.
  "Hello—Elena here.
  "Ruben's not home yet, General, but he called and Pepper's just arrived.
  "I see...yes, I'll tell him—but should you be doing this? Won't Pepper rebel? Times are changing, General.
  "Well... You know Pepper best, I'm sure. Bye now."

RUBEN APPROACHED THE FERRARI on Pepper's side. As he raised his sunglasses and bent from the waist for a better view inside the low-built vehicle, Pepper gnashed her teeth, slowly meeting his questioning gaze.

"This flashy tomato piece run out of juice?" he drawled.

Pepper shot Devlin a look asking for his help. He gave no sign of having noticed.

"We're not out of gas, Ruben," she replied tersely.

"So, ya got a flat tire then?" he asked, straightening and stepping back, eyes narrowed, to take in the Ferrari's two left tires.

Pepper nudged Devlin in the ribs. "Devlin." His name emerged low. Her hand dropped to his forearm, but when the heat of his flesh radiated through her fingers, she jerked away. "I can't tell him what we're doing here," she said out of the corner of her mouth.

"And whose fault is that?" he returned dryly.

"Hey, I admitted it was a bad idea."

Dev leaned across Pepper to address Ruben directly. "Nothing's wrong with the car, Rivera, except the air conditioner is cantankerous as all hell. Which I suspect is a result of the mechanical ability of your two brothers. Outside of that, your sister was just showing me the sights.''

Pepper pressed back in the seat trying to avoid contact with Dev in the close quarters, relieved to have him field Ruben's questions.

Ruben rotated in a half circle and back again, moving his thickset body from the waist up. ''Helluva pretty spot you picked, kid.'' His shrug along with his amused tone stated clearly enough what he really thought.

Pepper caught her lip between her teeth. How was it that Ruben had a way of making her feel guilty even when she wasn't?

Dev closed his eyes and massaged his brow. He'd forgotten the spartan landscape. He followed Ruben's gaze, and sure enough, there was not one thing on the stark horizon to warrant further comment. Dev decided it was time to close the subject. ''I thought you had an afternoon docket to preside over, Judge, and if that canceled, I distinctly remember your saying you were going to lift a few beers at your favorite drinking establishment.''

Ruben touched his forehead in a quick salute, raising a worn gray Stetson and resettling it more firmly on his head. ''Well, my cases were postponed. When I called Elena to let her know you were on the way, she suggested none too gently that I get my butt home. She reminded me about tonight's fiesta.'' He patted Smedley. ''Nice hound.''

Pepper leaned out of the window, craning her neck to see him. ''A fiesta... Oh, Ruben! Why didn't you tell us? What's it for?''

Her brother shifted his hat again and muttered half under his breath. ''Hell, you ever known Elena to need a reason to throw a fiesta?'' He shook his head ruefully and kicked the toe of one boot against the Ferrari's back tire. ''Right afterward, the ranchers are getting together for a little javelina roundup. You two wanna come along?''

Pepper drummed her fingers on the dash. ''Roundup? Don't you mean a hunt, Ruben?''

He gave a snort of disgust. "No. I mean a roundup. Kind of hard for all us oldtimers to adjust to the idea, but lately the Fish and Game Commission are relocating those critters."

Dev asked in a low tone—too low for Ruben to hear, "What kind of a roundup? Is it animal, vegetable or mineral?"

"Hav-a-lee-na," Pepper enunciated, rolling her eyes. "Wild pig in laymen's terms."

"Wild pig! The kind they cook in a pit? Like at a luau?"

"Hardly," she scoffed. "They're tough as tanned shoe leather. Mostly the little beasties multiply like wildfire and ruin crops. If you don't like fishing, I can almost guarantee you won't like grubbing around out in the wilds for javelina."

"Why are they relocating them?"

"Beats me," she said with a shrug. "You'll have to ask Ruben."

"What are you two whisperin' about?" Ruben rested an arm on the open window, then straightened quickly, making a grab for his Stetson as the tall crown brushed the roof edge, knocking the hat askew. "How about if we continue this stimulating conversation out at the ranch where we can have an ice-cold *cerveza* in hand?"

"*Cerveza* is beer," Pepper supplied at Dev's dubious look as Ruben continued.

"Maybe you two crazies see some beauty out here, but I'm just plain hot." Ruben wiped the sweat from his brow with the sleeve of his shirt, adding emphasis to his mocking tone.

Pepper saw it as a chance to keep from facing Devlin. "Great idea, Ruben. Maybe Major Wade would like to ride with you. Your air-conditioning alone will be a treat, and you can point out the historic landmarks better."

"Oh, sure, Pepper," Ruben returned sarcastically, "there are so many historic landmarks on this cow path. Let's all hightail it to the ranch and I'll check your air. You should have known better than to trust an amateur like Mike. And

Pete's mechanical ability has always been limited to filling a gas tank.''

Pepper looked at the dog who was again draped over Devlin's left shoulder. She laid one hand on his shaggy head and said as matter-of-factly as possible, ''Smedley needs a change, too. He can keep me company in the front seat.'' Smedley turned to look at her and yawned.

Shifting in his seat, Dev threw open the door and stretched his long legs outside. ''I think riding with Ruben is a good idea. He can tell me more about these wild pigs. You and Smedley are having too much fun on this trip— what with treeing tabby cats and rousing skunks. I think I'll concentrate on pigs.'' Sliding from the car, Dev chuckled.

''Devlin, wait! Don't you dare mention either of those incidents to Ruben.'' She lunged across the seat to block his slamming the car door.

Ruben had already boarded the truck, and Pepper found herself shouting ineffectually at Dev's broad back. He merely waved over one shoulder without turning.

''Darn you, Devlin Wade!''

Smedley wiggled between the two seats, helping himself to Dev's vacant one and pressing his nose to the window. He barked sharply when Ruben's green pickup started with a rough sputter.

''Oh, be quiet. Just remember who called you an unruly beast a few days ago. But if you still smelled like skunk I'd let him have you.''

Smedley whined, looking expectantly over one shoulder through a sliver of black eye nearly hidden beneath a curtain of tangled fur.

''I didn't mean to take out my frustrations on you, boy,'' Pepper said softly, pulling her fingers absentmindedly through the moplike strands at the ends of the dog's drooping ears. Then she slowly reached toward the silver key, still lodged in the ignition.

''There's just something about Devlin Wade that sends me into a tailspin. I haven't done one predictable thing since I met him.''

The Ferrari roared to life under her hand. "Maybe it wasn't such a good idea, after all—letting those two hooligans ride together, getting acquainted." She turned a sober eye on the dog. "Ruben's always excelled in cross-examination."

She let the pickup lead the way onto the main road, following at a discreet distance. "Papa always points out my biggest problem is foot-in-mouth disease and in this case, he's right." She groaned aloud. "Oh, Smedley. Whatever would I have done if Devlin had taken me at my word? Living with him..." Pepper's cheeks burned just thinking about the implications. "And he said I was too much a woman, Smedley. I wish he'd tell my family that. They treat me like a fourteen-year-old girl, and I'm tired of that."

Smedley barked sharply, circling three times before flopping on Devlin's seat. He panted, his tongue hanging out.

"Well, it's nice to have you agree." She made a face at him.

Lost in thought, Pepper drove mechanically, following the green pickup through rote turns. All too soon in her estimation, the Ferrari passed under the shadowed curve of a finely wrought iron arch leading to Ruben's hacienda. The logical part of Pepper's brain told her she should be thankful Devlin had turned her down, but the purely emotional part struggled with wondering what was wrong with her because he had.

By the time she guided the car to a stop in Ruben's brick courtyard, Major Wade's callous rejection had taken on all the characteristics of one of life's most embarrassing moments.

Wanting—needing—to extend her solitude a bit longer in order to escape Devlin Wade's potent masculinity and her own erratic feelings, Pepper dawdled getting out of the car. Fortunately for her the carved oak doors to Ruben's elegant home burst open, and four of her five rowdy nieces and nephews flew to smother their favorite aunt and her canine companion in welcoming kisses. If only for a moment, her worries fell away as Pepper hugged each one. Carried aloft on the happy laughter of Ruben's and Elena's warm, close-knit family, she began to feel more relaxed.

"You been on a working ranch before, Wade?" Ruben asked, giving a hand with their dufflebags.

"Never that I—" Dev stopped in midsentence and stared raptly at Pepper's changed expression. With the children, her laughter sounded spontaneous, eager. He resumed speaking in a huskier tone of voice, having completely missed Ruben's thoughtful study of him. "We moved a lot with the military. Spent most of the time in Europe in base housing. We were more likely to have tanks and missiles on our back forty."

"I'm glad Pop was based in Sierra Vista for so many years. A small town makes it easier to settle in, raise a family. You don't know what you missed. Take Pepper now—she belongs here."

"Yes," Dev answered, and he returned his longing gaze to Pepper and the children. "Yes, I can see that she does."

When Pepper did look Dev's way, the two men were deep in conversation. Her lightheartedness was quickly replaced by a flicker of despair. What must he think of her now? And when had she begun to care what Devlin Wade thought? She didn't know, but the awareness was sobering.

RUBEN'S WIFE, ELENA, bustled through the door, bringing with her an aura of charm and warmth Dev liked immediately. It had nothing to do with the fact that the dark-haired woman was juggling an array of ice-cold drinks. It was more the teasing twinkle in sable eyes, framed by genuine and undisguised laugh lines. Though it might also have had something to do with her easy acceptance of him, a total stranger, as her sister-in-law's traveling companion. Especially when her husband had been taking every opportunity to point out the differences between them.

"That your dog or Pepper's our kids are manhandling?" Elena looked at him and smiled, extending the tray she held.

Dev laughed with her, clutching his heart and feigning a look of pain before he took a long pull on the icy beer. He answered her with a teasing question of his own. "Do I look like the kind of man who would own that bedraggled mountain of fur?"

Elena took her time to assess him thoroughly. "Probably not. You look more like the German Shepherd type," she murmured, turning to watch Pepper toss a ball around with her brood.

Dev stopped smiling, his gaze coming to rest on Pepper. A subtle intertwining of innocence and sensuality sent strange prickles along his arms. "More like a Snoopy beagle, I'd say." He grinned lopsidedly, meeting Elena's eyes again. Though nothing further was said, he knew they weren't talking about the ownership of dogs anymore. Instead, their banter had assumed an intensely personal significance. He couldn't explain the tenderness he felt just watching Pepper. He wanted to be angry, had already admitted being disappointed—so it made no sense at all. Still his gaze didn't waver.

"Enough small talk," Ruben broke in gruffly. "I'm going to give the major a tour of the ranch. I promised to show him the string of Arabians I'm trying to build up."

"No, you don't, Ruben Rivera," Elena scolded. "First, get them settled in the guest rooms. After that, you can finish filling the luminaria bags with sand, followed by cleaning the swimming pool, followed by—"

"Okay, okay!" Ruben said. "You've made your point, slave driver. I knew I should have gone to Angel's." He rolled his eyes, throwing a pained expression Elena's way. "Inasmuch as we're expecting a full house for the next few days, Simon Legree, you'll need to spell it out—which rooms you want to give them?"

Chasing after a ball that had overshot its mark, Pepper, still flushed from her exertion, skidded into their midst just as Ruben asked his wife about rooms.

Holding her breath, she fixed Dev with a wary look, waiting for him to fill Ruben in on how she'd suggested they use one room, not two.

Elena greeted her sister-in-law warmly, taking no notice of Pepper's distress. She offered Pepper a frosty bottle of mineral water from the tray as she admonished her husband, "I declare, Ruben, if it takes you this long to make a simple decision over rooms, how long does it take you to hand down a verdict in court?" Snatching one duffle from his hands, she waved him away. "You and the major go! Pepper and I will see to these bags."

"We won't need rooms." Devlin tore his gaze away from Pepper. "If we stay after tonight, we'll be testing the cots. But could you tell me, do you have a lake close by?" He smiled teasingly at Pepper.

Pepper choked on her drink. She accepted a pat on the back from Elena, ignoring Ruben's raised brows. She sent Devlin a warning glance, which he received and acknowledged with a throaty chuckle.

"No need for any more of this palavering," Ruben said firmly. "We'll be traveling tonight to meet up with the Fish and Game transport trucks. We need to start tracking the javelina before the sun comes up. And there's no question of you two not staying, Wade. We've been lookin' forward to this visit with Pepper since Pop called."

"That reminds me!" Elena snapped her fingers, breaking into Ruben's conversation. "Raul called just before you got home. He wants to talk with you soon. Sounded like he's got another bee in his bonnet."

Ruben looked thoughtful. "With Pop I'd say it's more like a hornets' nest."

"Why is Papa calling you so much, Ruben? He hates making telephone calls." Pepper's tone was suspicious.

"Come on, Wade." Ruben motioned with his beer. "If we don't get out of here, Elena will add more work to my list."

"Ruben!" Pepper set her bottle back on the tray. "You're evading my question. I was intending to ask you about this when we were alone, but Miguel said some pretty disturbing things. He suggested that Papa engineered this trip." She bit her lower lip. "Miguel is such a practical joker...I mean, Papa wouldn't really have called General Wade and...and...well you know!" She turned beet red, refusing to look at Devlin.

"Why don't you quit worrying, Pepper." Ruben scowled. "This time Pop got a little carried away in his matchmaking." Though Ruben was speaking to his sister, it seemed his black look and belligerence were aimed at Devlin. "I still have connections in the army," he boasted, implying distinct threat. "And I'm not nearly so trusting as Pop when it comes to welcoming someone into our family with open arms. Maybe by now Pop will have changed his tune. Maybe when he really reads the copy of someone's transfer papers my buddy sent him."

Until Ruben's last barb, Devlin had been listening to the exchange between brother and sister with detached amusement. Now he took a step toward the rough-hewn man, an edge of anger replacing idle interest. "So Judge Rivera has been holding his own little kangaroo court? How convenient."

Elena hurried over, took her husband's empty beer bottle and asked if either of them wanted another.

Each man seemed reluctant to back down from the grim staring match. Ruben was first to give ground. He shrugged and reached for the frosty bottle Elena offered. "Later," he muttered, giving the cap a vigorous twist. Turning on his heel, he stalked away.

Devlin refused the drink. "I'm not much on beer," he explained. "My taste runs more to a dry chardonnay—but thanks anyway."

Elena picked up the tray and sighed loudly.

"What was all that about?" Pepper demanded. "Has this whole family taken leave of its senses?"

"Your Pop isn't the only Cupid you'll have to deal with this time, Pepper. I think you should tell the lot of them to let you do your own looking."

"Are you coming, Major?" Ruben called from the doorway of the hacienda. "I'm sure they didn't teach you how to fill luminaria bags in Washington. Elena, why don't you give Major Wade a lesson?"

Elena joined her husband at the door and pushed him none too gently inside. Pepper and Devlin stood facing one another without anyone to intervene. She shifted her weight to one hip, dug the toe of a sneaker into the rough edge of terra cotta brick and watched the children chase circles around Smedley.

"I don't exactly know what to say in defense of my relatives, Major," she murmured. "Normally they're nice people. They just feel strongly about family." And as she stood watching the antics of her oldest brother's lively offspring, she was struck for the first time by a longing to have a family of her own. It was a new, disturbing emotion.

Reacting to the tenderness he could see softening Pepper's delicate features, Devlin touched the tip of her nose with his index finger. "Let's leave it until after the fiesta." The look of surprise creeping into her eyes made him feel suddenly self-conscious. But he couldn't resist adding, "Don't forget you still owe me—and I'm not talking about the fifty bucks."

Pepper felt her face flush and bent to inspect the red dust staining her white sneakers. "Go let Elena show you how to fix luminaria, but watch what you say around her, too. She's been known to do her share of matchmaking. Still, if you've never been to a fiesta, Dev, you'll enjoy this one. Ruben and Elena put on a good spread. Good food, good music and plenty of beer."

"Now why would the proud new owner of Wade's Wine Works get excited over a fiesta where the main beverage is beer?" Dev shook his head and walked away, still chuckling to himself. Pepper joined in, not registering what he'd said. She did puzzle over why, at times, the major looked more like a civilian than a military man. . . .

THE PARTY WAS in full swing before Pepper saw Devlin again. One of Elena's sisters had brought a simple, white, peasant-style dress for her to wear, as she hadn't come prepared for a fiesta.

Devlin, she soon learned, had purchased more at the store in Larkspur than the shirt and shorts he'd worn earlier. His fiesta attire was a form-fitting pair of white slacks and a loose cotton shirt in a kind of jungle print in varying shades of blue. With his dark hair and tan, Pepper found it most appealing. She felt the white dress left her ghostly by comparison, and lacking her usual flair.

To Dev, Pepper looked stunning. The fiery highlights of her red hair shimmered in the flickering lights from the many luminarias, setting her enticingly apart from the other women present, though many of them were undeniably pretty. A fire opal left to him in Grandmother Wade's will would be the perfect gem for her, he suddenly decided. The intrusive thought hit hard, causing him a moment of distress.

Devlin set his beer down on the nearest redwood table with a thud, abruptly ending his conversation with one of the local ranchers. His heartbeat matched the tempo of the resonant flamenco guitars. The night was made for romance, and he had only one woman in mind. Tonight he would forget their differences and concentrate on enjoying the new experience of a fiesta.

Across the room, the curve of Pepper's golden shoulders graced by the soft folds of her white dress drew him to her side. So intent was he on reaching her that he failed to see Ruben stop, touch her elbow and introduce her to a tall dignified man wearing a Western-style suit, tailor-made to fit. Dev was surprised when she was swept from his line of vision, only to reappear, whirling on the crowded dance floor with a stranger.

As he blinked and his heart settled into a more manageable rhythm, he saw that Ruben was the only person left standing in the corner. He also saw that the judge was very nearly glowing from the amount of *cerveza* he'd already consumed. Dev had a sudden urge to wipe the sappy, satisfied grin off Ruben's face.

"Oh, hello, Wade." Ruben swayed to the music. "They make a fine-lookin' couple, don't you agree?" Not waiting for a response, Ruben turned to face the swirling couple again.

"Who is he?" Dev growled.

The harshness of Dev's tone seemed to amuse his host. "Neighbor of ours by the name of Ken Boyd. Just bought the thousand acres adjoining my ranch. Has plenty of cash. Owns a second, bigger spread down along the gulf. I've heard it said he's into oil, too."

"He's too old for her," Dev said, feeling his jaw tighten. "How old is he, anyway? I'm surprised he's not already taken if he's such a great catch."

Ruben lifted one brow. He turned to the table behind him, plunged his hand into an ice chest and pulled out a can of beer. Then he snapped off the top and motioned Dev to help himself. "Ken's a widower." Ruben drank deeply. "And I'm not one to hold much with stereotyping. Can't rightly say there's such a thing as too old or too young when it comes to lovers."

"Lovers!" Devlin spat the word. He'd refused the beer when Ruben first offered; now thinking better of it, he jerked the cap off a bottle of mellow Dos Eques. Never much of a drinker, he suddenly felt the need to strike common ground with Pepper's brother. His instincts told him this man was a far greater threat than the blustering Mike.

Ruben laughed wickedly. People turned to look, including Pepper and her partner who were circling close to the edge of the dance floor. She'd been chatting pleasantly with Ken Boyd, but when her gaze met Devlin's measured disapproval, she pressed her lips tightly together, turning her head away.

"A man might take you for a jealous lover yourself, Major Wade, the way you sound." Ruben leaned toward Dev, his jaw squared, the muscles in his neck and arms bunched and tense. "How about it? You sleepin' two on a cot this trip, amigo?"

Dev stepped back, rocked by an overwhelming desire to physically separate himself from Ruben's harsh probe. Protective of his new and still untried feelings for this man's sister, Devlin was suddenly struck by an awareness that Ruben Rivera was not nearly so drunk as he'd first thought. This heavy-handed sibling was simply using the glow of ale as a crafty ploy to provoke him.

As Devlin's heated stare followed the couple twirling around the floor, their bodies swaying in time to the throb of the sensuous music, he considered out-and-out lying— telling Ruben what he expected to hear, what he'd been in-sinuating all day. Should he allow Ruben to think his sister had already been seduced by Dev Wade, the big bad wolf? It might stake a claim. And it would be easy to do, because Dev knew beyond a doubt that *he* longed to be the one holding her in his arms this very minute. Yet he only con-sidered the option of lying for one heartbeat. Anything less than the truth would compromise Pepper and he wouldn't— couldn't—do that to her.

Finding that he cared what Pepper's family thought of him left Dev feeling edgy. His jaw stiffened to match Rub-en's. "If the opportunity presented itself on this outing, Judge, I didn't take it." He let go of the words slowly, matching his harsh glare to Ruben's demanding one. "Just maybe the next time you call me amigo, you'll realize you should mean it. And just maybe you should go back to your army buddy and get the truth." Slamming his bottle on the table, Dev spun on one heel and strode from the patio, not breathing again until he was immersed in the outer ring of darkness.

Once the warm evening closed around him, he grew calmer. Minutes later he realized that he'd act no differ-ently if he had a sister. That fact salved his ego, allowing him to return to the well-lighted patio. He focused all his energy on keeping Pepper in sight, even though watching her float from the arms of one man to another left him discontented. Always, it seemed, she drifted back to the rancher, Ken Boyd.

Certain that Pepper wouldn't welcome his intrusion, Dev refrained from cutting in. From the sidelines he watched. He waited. And he suffered in silence, not wanting to pressure her. Ruben also kept his distance and that was fine, too. Devlin might not blame Ruben, but neither could he forgive the slur cast on his character. And that old, empty restless feeling was sharper, more pronounced among the music, the laughter, the sights and smells of the fiesta. When at last he caught Pepper's eye, Dev knew unequivocally that it was time for them to share a dance.

Pepper sensed it, too. She had only appeared to grow more carefree as the party progressed. Each time a dance ended and a new one began, she was confident Devlin would seek her out. Each time some other man claimed her, her heart sank a little. The carefree facade was meant to buoy her own spirits.

She had kept a watchful eye on Devlin's progress. Once, when he left the patio unexpectedly, she'd wanted to dash after him, but couldn't leave Ruben's friend, Ken Boyd, standing alone on the dance floor. She felt bad for the charming older man, knowing that her brother was trying to fob her off on him, and she felt as if she'd lost some important link with Ruben. But looking at Devlin now, she felt on the brink of discovering something new. The last dance of the evening had just been announced. If Devlin didn't claim her for it, she'd ask him.

Resolutely she moved toward him, not even pausing to thank her last partner.

"So you saved me a dance, after all?" Dev's voice was deep, rough around the edges.

Pepper's eyes held his without wavering. "You could have had them all for the asking."

He didn't want to consider the portent of that remark. To avoid it, he gathered her close, sighing when her soft curves met his firmer contours. For just a moment, he closed his eyes, breaking the visual link, enjoying her only by the exquisite sense of touch. "The soles of your shoes must be nearly worn out from dancing." His voice shook slightly, as did the arms holding her close.

Not wanting anything to alter the mood she'd created in her mind, she hesitated to ask why he'd not danced a single dance. She murmured something noncommittal and savored being tucked tight against Dev's chest. Still, some nuance, some vibration whispered through her—intuition, perhaps.

"What were you and Ruben discussing so intently right after the fiesta started?" Pepper levered a space between them and tried to read his eyes. The luminaria were burning low and the flickering light only reached his chin. She tilted her head higher. Their feet barely moved across the smooth tile and they were almost standing still, yet neither seemed to notice.

Dev hadn't expected to be so honest with her. He was simply enjoying these moments together, holding her. He didn't want to let her go and was more surprised than she at his own gruff words. "Your brother wanted to know if we were sleeping together on this trip."

Pepper caught her breath sharply. Her eyes refused to meet his. Involuntarily she backed away, lowering her lashes. "I see. And you couldn't wait to tell him what I suggested—and did you also tell him how you threw the suggestion back in my face? By morning, I should imagine both our families will hear about it." She burned with shame at the way she'd hoped to taunt the well-meaning matchmakers.

Devlin felt her accusation like a slap. The fact that she could think him capable of such a betrayal added fuel to Ruben's insult and shattered the mood for him. Letting his arm drop from around her shoulder, he retained hold of her hand. He turned abruptly, then strode off the dance floor, pulling her roughly in his wake. He didn't react to the startled looks of other dancers or bystanders, nor did he stop until they were well outside the lighted courtyard.

From all sides came sounds of the party breaking up. Rising above the din, Ruben's voice could be heard calling for a meeting of the javelina hunters.

Pepper hung back, pulling against his grip, and when he stopped, she was breathless. "Devlin, what is the matter with you?" She jerked away and one hand came up to rub her wrist. "There's no need for you to suffer Ruben's wrath just because I said something without thinking it through. We'll leave now, head for the base, and I'll take my lumps from my father."

Dev leaned toward her, backing her against the rough cool adobe of the hacienda. "Ruben's wrath and your father's be damned. You and I are going on that abominable outing, my charming general's daughter, so Ruben can pass the word that I'll not be manipulated by him, or by your father, or by mine." Dev paused to check his watch. "And I'll give you exactly fifteen minutes to be at Ruben's meeting, dressed for hunting piggies, or we'll damn well go with you dressed as you are." Deriving a certain amount of pleasure from the shocked look in her eyes, Devlin stalked away, wondering why he never seemed to find any middle ground with this woman.

Stunned by his outburst, she watched him storm off. A brief flash of sheet lightning lit the western sky, followed by a muffled distant roll of thunder. *There he goes giving orders again,* she thought, mustering a scowl. Well, major or no, he was a novice when it came to scouring ravines for javelina. We'll just see how good *he* is at taking orders. Piggies, indeed!

In the distance a second round of lightning skittered brokenly, and a warning shiver snaked up her spine. Chin held high, Pepper ambled slowly toward the house, absolutely determined that it would take her at least *twenty* minutes to change her clothes.

CHAPTER NINE

THURSDAY MORNING, LARKSPUR, New Mexico
Rrring.

"Elena? It's Maria. Do you think we'd better get serious and plan for a wedding this time?"

"You think the spark's there, too? Wanna meet me in Tucson? See what we can find to wear?"

PEPPER FOUND HERSELF both dreading and looking forward to meeting Devlin in the corral. Her steps barely touched the polished red brick of the courtyard as she moved beneath lacy Paloverde branches. Some part of her still lingered in a sensual cocoon wrought by the fading flamenco guitars and the high-pitched symphony of cicadas; a part that blended with the memory of how good his holding her had felt during one brief dance. It was difficult to stay angry, feeling this soft warmth inside.

But a point was a point. After exactly twenty-one minutes, Pepper slipped through the gate expecting to see the old Devlin Wade, assuming he'd fall back into his role of military officer. But he was again dressed in civilian garb, wearing a chambray shirt, soft cotton chinos and Western-style boots. He looked wonderful. He must have spent a fortune at Estebar's. Pepper had difficulty concentrating on Ruben's instructions.

The hunting party was large and most members were well acquainted. Much joking and good-natured ribbing was going on. Ruben's voice climbed above the chatter. "Okay everyone, listen up. We're going to divide you into teams. We have a lot of oldtimers, but plenty of new faces. And I have here a roster." The crowd quieted. "The Fish and

Game Department wants a representative with each group. We're going to trap the javelina, and Fish and Game will transport them to a new location." Quickly he read off the names as assigned. In the end, he'd deliberately paired Pepper with Ken Boyd and Devlin with another group. "Any questions?" He didn't look at Pepper as he asked.

Ruben's intent was easy to read. Thoroughly angry with her brother's manipulations, not to mention his rudeness toward Devlin, Pepper made up her mind to outmaneuver him.

"Ruben," she called as the throng began to split up, "change Devlin into my group, will you?" She smiled as Ruben blustered. "He and I will take the Ferrari to the point where we transfer to horses. Major Wade is, after all, my guest."

Dev looked surprised by her announcement. He'd thought she'd be angry with him. He'd been sure of it when she strolled in late.

"I have plenty of room in my Jimmy," offered Boyd. "You're both welcome to ride with me. I'll take our game rep, too."

"Thanks anyway," Pepper cut in, watching Ruben scowl again. "We won't be returning to the ranch. When the roundup's over, we'll go on to the base. And we have a dog to think about, you know." Turning away, Pepper paused outside the corral to wait for Devlin. He was talking to the couple Ruben had teamed him up with and she supposed he was explaining.

Pepper felt good about standing up to Ruben. The thought of spending time alone with Devlin on the way to the site felt good, too—a feeling she couldn't easily explain, but one she wanted time to explore.

Devlin walked briskly through the paddock, vaulted the corral fence and fell in step, sliding his arm around her waist. Leaning close to her ear he muttered, "I owe you one for standing up to Ruben. Those folks take this javelina business seriously. They were pretty relieved not to be stuck with a greenhorn." He smiled down at her. "Are you sure you want me tagging along? I get the idea it's a little tougher than filling luminaria bags with sand. I suspect Ruben's out to teach me a lesson."

Heat prickled along Pepper's arm as Devlin's fingers accidentally brushed the underside. "I shouldn't do you any favors, the way you try to boss me around. And Ruben means well. He just—" She stopped midsentence. How did she explain having a family determined to marry her off? "Elena's father and mine had Ruben's marriage all arranged before they were out of high school. Times change, but Papa doesn't. Since my brothers helped raise me, they tend to order, not ask— Uh-oh! Here's Ruben now."

Dev tightened his arm around Pepper's waist. "Let's hit the road before he comes up with a new plan." Pepper pulled loose and dashed to the kitchen for a paper sackful of leftover treats, while Dev waited impatiently. Then she slipped back into his hold, and half running, he hurried her along. They were winded when they reached the car. Smedley, tied to a nearby tree, woke up and began barking. By the time she threw Dev the car keys and the three of them had piled into the Ferrari, they were laughing like conspirators.

"Why do I suddenly feel like the Clyde half of Bonnie and Clyde?" he joked. Gunning the motor, he shot off amid a squeal of rubber. "You have too many brothers in law enforcement, Pepper. I don't relish spending a night in Ruben's jail."

Pepper poked Dev in the ribs teasingly. "Just make it to the end of Ruben's lane and turn left. One hundred yards and you're out of his jurisdiction. We'll be in Arizona. Free!"

She sounded so serious Dev eased up on the accelerator. "I was only kidding," he said dryly. "We are headed in the right direction to go on this roundup, aren't we?"

"Relax, Major, I was talking about your speeding. Ruben won't charge you with kidnapping. He's just unhappy because I let him know he can't keep choosing men for me. Your sterling reputation is still intact." She lifted her chin and said frankly, "Devlin, don't get me wrong. I really love my brothers. I didn't make that earlier suggestion—the one about our living together—to alienate them. I just wanted them to back off, to let me live my own life, make my own choices. They've all had the freedom to sow wild oats, at least if they wanted to."

The car slowed at the end of Ruben's long drive. Devlin hesitated only an instant before turning left and heading for the dark checkpoint marking the Arizona state line.

"Is that what you're using me for? To help sow your wild oats?"

Pepper sighed. Her gaze left Dev's unyielding features to follow faint traces of lightning silhouetting the southernmost tip of the Chiricahua Mountains. The distant storm and the roundup seemed miles away from the confinement of the car and Dev's lingering disapproval. She steeled herself, determined to ask him something that had been bothering her. "If you could just tell me why you got so mad when I made that suggestion. I mean, Pete heard that you squired beautiful ladies to parties in Washington—enough to get your picture in the paper. Your friend Zach told Mike you were a man about town. I was just wondering what you find objectionable about me?" She felt his eyes burn into her, but not for the world would she look up to meet his gaze. Instead she watched her fingers pleat little folds in the hem of her shirt.

The checkpoint loomed to their left, delaying Dev's answer. A sleepy guard waved them through after a series of mechanical questions. Dev lifted one hand from the wheel and passed it slowly over his mouth and jaw before he spoke.

"There isn't a single thing objectionable about you, Pepper...and maybe that's part of the problem." He drummed his fingers on the steering wheel. "I'm no saint, but I don't use women and I don't like being used. I told Ruben and Mike as much." Devlin looked away, shifting his weight in the seat. "All my life I've been groomed to fit Gentleman Win's image of the perfect officer." His jaw tensed as he turned toward her. "I made rank on my own terms, but he was always in the background, ready to pull strings. It was a constant source of jealousy on the part of my peers—the underlying reason I'm being shipped to your father's base in the first place. But then, you know all about that already." His voice held a bitter edge.

Pepper strained to see him in the darkness. His lips were set in a stubborn line, his shoulders squared. "Devlin, believe it or not, you're talking in riddles. From the outset of this trip you've assumed I have some classified information about you. I assure you, before walking into your father's party, I'd never heard of Major Devlin Wade."

Devlin stretched his leg and stomped on the gas. The Ferrari whined, kicking in extra power for the long climb into Apache Pass. Now the sheer cliffs hid all traces of lightning. With the absence of stars and other cars on the desolate roadway, the Ferrari's headlights glowed eerily. As the highway curved south, one-hundred-year-old saguaro cacti hovered in small clusters like lonely sentinels.

Devlin wasn't sure he believed her. After all, his father, her father and Ruben all knew about the Huston mess. Something was afoot, something planned by those men, and he had little reason to trust any of them. His integrity had suffered at Candy Huston's hands, and integrity was the one thing he'd always made sure belonged to him, untouched and unsullied as he climbed reluctantly up Gentleman Win's ladder. If Pepper didn't know, then she was the only one who didn't. Maybe it was better left that way. Sharing confidences had never been easy for him. Yet there she sat, quietly waiting, her warm scent seeping into his pores.

Painfully, feeling exposed, he said at last, "A certain officer at the Pentagon coveted my job. He set me up, then spread a nasty rumor about me and the young wife of General Huston. Mistakenly I counted on my innocence, and the lady to tell the truth. Unfortunately I sensed too late that she needed me to cover her affair with the officer, who needed my job to keep her in high style. It all gets very sticky. The real irony here is that he would have gotten my job anyway. I'd already planned to resign my commission, just as soon as I found a way to tell my father. I bought a little wine shop and an old farmhouse in Virginia. This was after realizing I'd stayed in the wrong mold for so many years just to please him. When you proposed more deceit, this time involving me with a general's daughter, well, I'm afraid it was a familiar story to me. And it's not my reputation I'm concerned about, Mary Kathleen. It's yours.''

Pepper's heart plummeted. Her throat was too tight for her to make any comment. As she digested his story, she felt shame again for her thoughtless suggestion and was relieved to spot the turnoff. ''Turn here.'' She pointed and braced herself for the car's sudden swerve. One sentence flashed on and off inside her brain like a neon sign. *Dev is planning to resign his commission.* And all this time, she'd assumed he was just another officer on the climb.

''I didn't know any of that, Dev. If I had, it might have changed some things...'' Her voice trailed off.

''Are we close to arriving?'' Devlin's brow furrowed. ''Ruben sure fixed the air this time. Turn it down, will you?''

Pepper shut the unit off as she answered, ''The javelina are in those foothills. They travel in herds and ruin the farmland you see along here.'' She inclined her head to the left. But before he could look, she burst out, ''How can you leave the army? You can't be far from your twenty-year retirement. What about all the years you've already invested? What if your...wine shop doesn't work out?'' Once she'd spoken, Pepper feared he'd resent her bluntness.

Dev guided the Ferrari down a narrow road and pulled into the clearing she'd indicated. Shutting off the engine, he leaned his head against the headrest. They were first to arrive.

''Do you think military is synonymous with security?'' Devlin's tone was brittle. ''I'm surprised you haven't had your pick of officers between Pete and your father. If they want you married, why aren't you? Why all this cloak-and-dagger stuff on the part of your family?'' Reaching out, Devlin grasped her shoulders, turning her, making her face him.

Pepper arched away, straining against his hold.

''Not an officer—never,'' she whispered. ''Pete doesn't know—none of them do. They just want me in a nest. It's Rivera tradition.''

"Why not an officer? Level with me, Pepper," Dev pursued relentlessly. "I told you the truth. The least you can do is give me honesty in return. Don't forget we're in this together—whatever it is."

She lowered her chin to her chest, closing her eyes. "I fell for a captain once and swore never again. It wasn't love really. But I didn't know that then. Anyway, he neglected to tell me he had a fiancée back in Ohio. I used my father's name to help him move in the right circles. I wangled invitations to social functions Papa held. I made a fool of myself over him and he threw it all back in my face. He took his upgrade and his new wife to a four-year duty station in Germany." Pepper feared saying it aloud might shatter her tight control. Amazingly the bands that had been squeezing off her breath eased a bit.

Devlin's jaw worked spasmodically. His fingers tightened on her arms, then relaxed, his hands falling loosely by his sides. Pepper huddled against the corner between her seat and the door. She gazed at him helplessly. Why didn't he say something? Why didn't he flail her with accusations as she had flailed herself? But then, to be honest, Pepper didn't think she could bear it if Devlin viewed her old indiscretion in the same light as he did General Huston's wife and her manipulations. So she sat, silent and wooden as Devlin withdrew. He threw open the car door, awakened Smedley, and with the dog disappeared into the purple shadows of a desert dawn.

Pepper forced her limbs to react. Stiff fingers moved to unbuckle an uncooperative seat belt. And when she twisted in the seat to inspect it, salty tears clouded her vision. She couldn't blame him for thinking she'd been trying to trap the captain. Or for rejecting yesterday's impetuous suggestion, especially after his experience with that general's wife. Her fingers finally managed to work the buckle. She almost tumbled from the car when Devlin jerked open the passenger door without warning. She gasped as he pulled her from the car and settled his warm lips over her parted ones, absorbing not only the noise of her surprise, but the moistness of her tears.

His kiss was at first demanding. Then it softened, stroked, then grew desperately rough again. Pulling away a moment, he clasped her to his chest, buried his lips in the spicy scent near her ear and murmured, "Ah, Pepper, we're quite a pair aren't we? Life for army brats isn't as easy as everyone thinks."

Pepper's knees refused to support her. Inside she felt warmth curl, coil, grow painfully hot and melting. Then she was urging his lips back to hers and returning his kisses.

His hands slid down her back, following the curve of her waist. His sigh was nearly a groan.

Pepper worked her palms beneath his shirt, reaching the warm expanse of his back. Reacting, not thinking, she nipped sharply at his lower lip. His groan deepened and its sensuous urgency seemed to surround her, seemed to echo from the very landscape.

The growl swelled, becoming ever louder, and Pepper felt Devlin shift away. She suddenly realized that Smedley's barking had begun to overpower the steady noise. Cold metal from the Ferrari's door handle replaced Devlin's warm palm on her back. With rude reality, Pepper settled down to earth.

"Great timing," muttered Devlin, eyeing a line of approaching vehicles. "In another ten minutes, I might have been guilty of lying to Ruben, after all." He tucked in his shirt, then helped Pepper straighten her own. Color rushed to her cheeks.

"You don't need to look guilty, Pepper. Nothing happened. Nothing," he repeated as the first in a cavalcade of pickups, horse trailers and four-by-fours reached the clearing.

Pepper still stared at him, her knees weak. Maybe for the major nothing had happened, but she felt otherwise. With Smedley at his heels, Dev struck out across the desert to meet Ruben's green pickup. She hadn't had proper time to sort out precisely what had changed in their relationship and that "nothing" of a kiss continued to plague Pepper as the group made preparations.

Ruben passed out water canteens and maps. This first trip was to be reconnaissance, as javelina tended to stake out and cover the same terrain. Tomorrow the plan was to go back with cages. Pepper only went through the motions, her mind consumed by the soul-searing kiss she had shared with Devlin.

He, on the other hand, appeared to be engrossed in each tiny detail. Not once during the entire process did he touch her or even look her way.

As the sun rose and dust devils kicked up, Pepper wondered what she'd ever found enjoyable about a hunt. The sleepless night and subsequent tension sapped her energy and skewed her priorities.

"You ride, Wade?" Pepper heard Ruben ask Devlin from the far side of a big bay gelding.

Pepper stirred from her lethargy long enough to intervene. "Give him Cinder, Ruben," she said.

"Tenderfoot, huh?" Ruben peered over the gelding and laughed. Others in the party were going through a routine of checking gear and mounting up. One member of each team was assigned to carry flares and a gun for emergencies. Ken Boyd volunteered to act for their team.

Devlin hooked his thumbs in his pant pockets, studying first Pepper, then Ruben's restless bay.

"I think I'll defer to the lady's decision," he remarked to Ruben. "She knows me pretty well." The smile he bestowed on her was tender.

Ruben caught the look and yanked the cinch with more vigor than necessary. Pepper heard the horse grunt. Or was it Ruben? She hid a wry smile.

"Pepper, you'll be riding an Arabian mare of Ken's. A real beauty. Strong and fast. Name's Isis. He bought her at the last auction. I'm jealous. Too bad I didn't see her first."

Even as Ruben spoke, Ken Boyd led two dancing Arabians from his horse trailer. Pepper couldn't help but admire the mare and the stallion. She'd always had a weakness for good horseflesh, and Boyd's Arabians were beauties.

As she ran a hand down the white mare's neck, she chanced to see Ruben's smug look and knew this was another of his railroad jobs. Someone ought to tell Ruben that it was the man, not the horse, that mattered when a woman fell in love, she thought, tight-lipped.

Love. The word entered her mind so easily. Flushing, she turned away, calling Smedley to heel. Her palms grew damp as she tied the dog securely to the bumper of Ruben's truck. "We can't let Smedley come," she said to Dev. "Javelina and dogs are natural enemies. We don't want a fight."

Love. The word surfaced again, overshadowing the conversation between the three men going on behind her. Questions without answers swirled inside her head. Did simply knowing that Devlin no longer climbed the military ladder shatter the wall she'd built around her heart? Why did it matter? She watched Kenneth Boyd ride toward her and accepted his offer of the white horse. Declining his help, she stepped lightly into the stirrup and vaulted neatly into the saddle.

Devlin guided his black mare close. "Impressive." He winked. "The Lone Ranger couldn't have done better. Maybe I should stay with Smedley. After all, I don't want to slow you down."

"What, and let Ruben win after I went to bat for you?" Isis suddenly reared on her hind legs and nipped at Devlin's mount. Pepper pulled her horse back.

Then Isis bolted and ran for a hundred yards before Pepper gained the upper hand. She choked up on the reins and got a firmer grip on the feisty horse with her knees, then motioned for Dev to join her. Pepper was disappointed when Kenneth Boyd and a dark-eyed woman of about thirty-five rode up beside him. A few minutes alone with Devlin would have been nice.

In the red-streaked sky overhead, a morning hawk circled majestically. To the east, the Chiricahua Mountains rose sharp and darkly rugged. But farther south a jagged flash of light splintered a blue-gray sky. Sonora, on the Mexican side of the border, was getting hit by a summer storm. Pepper gave it no more than a cursory thought. Her attention was focused not on the beauty of daybreak or the distant storm but on the attractive sight Devlin made, seated tall and straight on the gentle black mare.

"This is Rita Santos." Kenneth presented the woman to Pepper and Devlin. "She's our representative from Fish and Game."

Rita acknowledged them with a brief, apprehensive smile. "I hope that storm stays in Mexico, don't you?"

Boyd shrugged lightly, his gaze on Pepper's worried brow. "Ruben thought Rita would pair up nicely with Major Wade. She's not the experienced horsewoman you are, Pepper."

Pepper's look changed to one of chagrin. She'd have to hand it to Ruben—he didn't give up easily. Still, she had a trick or two of her own. She gave Rita a warm smile. "Being with Fish and Game, you must have some hot tips for trapping these little critters. Maybe you can ride ahead with Ken and fill him in, while I brief Devlin on the horse Ruben loaned him."

Rita brightened. "It'll be the other way around, I'm afraid. I'm in the process of changing careers—going from nursing into animal husbandry. I'm a trainee in the Fish and Game docent program. I heard Ruben say Kenneth was the javelina expert in this group. I'm actually planning to learn from him."

Boyd looked unsure for a moment and Pepper was afraid he'd decline. "Kenneth, you don't mind, do you?" She looped a hand beneath the bridle of Devlin's mount. "I really must explain some things about this horse." Rita shot her a grateful look before returning her gaze to Ken Boyd. So that's the way it was, Pepper mused. Rita Santos had a crush on Ruben's rancher friend. Pepper laughed a little to herself. Ruben would be furious.

"What's wrong with this horse?" Devlin's soft-spoken query broke into her amusement. "Does she imitate Pegasus when she sees a wild pig? I thought you were looking out for my best interests when you insisted Ruben give me this horse?"

"Nothing's wrong with Cinder," Pepper said, feeling self-conscious in Devlin's presence, and a little guilty now that she'd rearranged circumstances to suit herself. "Couldn't you see that Rita wanted to be alone with Kenneth Boyd?"

Devlin studied the couple up ahead. The soft thud of horses' hooves mixed with creaking leather and the occasional clank of metallic tack. Rita Santos was talking animatedly.

"Now who's matchmaking?" Dev searched her face wistfully as he teased. When Pepper's cheeks flamed, he grew serious. "Pepper, about the way I acted back in the car..." He paused, clearing his throat. She looked away, watching Ken and Rita disappear behind an enormous red boulder. Isis snorted and pranced, and they began to thread their way through fields of corn and lettuce.

"Look!" she exclaimed, not wanting to hear the apology lurking in his voice. "You can see how the javelina have torn up the soil rooting for food. They love lettuce. It's what we'll use to entice them into the cages tomorrow." Kicking Isis sharply in the rib cage, Pepper let her mare climb the steep path.

Whatever Devlin might have said was kept at bay as they spent the next few hours traversing the rugged terrain. At some point in the early afternoon they heard Ken Boyd's lusty shout.

"Javelina below!" His resonant call echoed off the narrow canyon walls, falling away after the next rise.

"Where are they?" Devlin craned his neck, looking all around.

"The javelina?" Pepper dug binoculars out of a saddle-bag. "Probably in the ravines along that lower ridge."

"Actually I meant Ken and Rita," he answered. "I can hear them, but I can't tell where they are."

"Now you know how Cochise and his band evaded the cavalry for so long," Pepper answered with a smile. "If the stories I've heard are true, the army could pass within ten feet of Cochise and his men without ever knowing they were there." She eased back in the saddle, letting Isis pick her way through the scattered boulders. The terrain had changed markedly, growing rugged.

Devlin followed her example. "This is a regular rat maze in here. One pile of red rocks looks like the next."

Rita's shrill voice sounded close by, then all at once farther away. It seemed to mock them by coming from several directions at once. Pepper's horse danced nervously. Then, rounding the crest of a promontory, they almost ran into the other couple.

Ken had taken the rifle from its scabbard. His stallion was crow-hopping along a narrow trail. Rita had her hands full keeping her Appaloosa gelding under control.

Devlin's gaze shifted to a shadowy movement in the canyon below. Almost immediately he was treated to his first look at javelina. The beasts were every bit as ugly as Ruben had described. Dark and grizzled and not nearly as fat as domestic pigs, the leathery animals grubbing about in the rocks were evil looking, enough to raise the hair along the back of his neck.

"I'd guess their leader to be that big black devil. See the one standing beside that twisted mesquite? He looks to be part razorback." Ken's voice rose excitedly. Looping the reins over his pommel, he lifted his rifle. "I say let's take him out."

"Put the gun away, Ken. Ruben said we were only to get a fix on them today," Pepper cautioned, urging her mare close to the edge of a sheer drop-off. She shaded her eyes against a splash of sunlight. "You have the gun in case of an emergency."

Ken lowered his rifle. "You're right, Pepper. I just got overzealous. I haven't seen a prize like that one in years." He laughed. "Once a hunter, always a hunter, I guess." He slid the rifle back into its case and reined in. "You game to get a closer look, Pepper? I think Wade should stay here with Rita. That isn't a trail for any tenderfoot."

Rita agreed readily. Devlin, however, said nothing. He just took the measure of the narrow switchback leading into the canyon.

"I don't know..." Pepper's horse was getting edgy, straining at the bit. But Ken didn't wait to hear her decision. He nudged his mount forward and the stallion's hooves hit the rocky slope. Horse and rider slid several feet before recovering their footing.

Pepper chewed on her lip as she gathered the reins tightly in her left hand.

"Don't go!" Devlin caught her elbow.

"Rule number one," she quoted. "Don't leave a partner alone. Javelina are small and therefore look inconsequential, but they can be deadly." Shaking off his hand, she directed Isis over the edge of the precipice.

Devlin hauled in a ragged breath. "No sense all of us being fools." He shot Rita a stern look. "You stay here on solid ground. I can't let her go without me."

Rita's dark eyes met his with understanding. She didn't answer, merely nodded her consent.

Dev's mount worked her way carefully down the trail, and he was doing fine until a shot rang out. Worry had him touching his heels to Cinder's ribs. The trail ahead took a sharp downturn. Neither Ken nor Pepper were in sight.

Around the next corner, the valley suddenly opened up and fanned out below. Devlin could see Ken in the lead position, standing in his stirrups, taking aim at a massive, snarling pig. His horse was backed tight against one wall in a box canyon. It seemed to Dev that Ken's only way out was past the javelina, now pawing the ground with sharp hooves. Urging Cinder closer, he could see the beast's crazed eyes and curling yellowed tusks.

Suddenly Ken's horse reared and leaped sideways to avoid the charging pig. The man was tossed from the saddle, falling hard against a rock. His rifle clattered down the canyon slope in a hail of smaller stones. The pig was momentarily distracted by the noise.

Pepper rode into the canyon from behind and reined in the delicate Arabian only yards from the downed man. Her movements drew the javelina's attention. Spinning, the pig changed tactics and rushed his new adversary with the speed of a wildcat. Isis reared, screeching. Fighting to control the terrified horse, Pepper lost her seat and landed in a clump of sagebrush. Unable to catch her breath, she watched as once more the pig whirled around and headed for the fallen Ken.

At the entrance to the canyon now, Devlin kicked his heels hard into the sides of Cinder's belly. She moved at one pace. Slow. He heard Ken Boyd's warning shouts mixed with the sound of his own heart thundering in his ears. Fear for Pepper's safety, a fear he could taste, drove him into the path of the pig.

With a firm yank, Devlin practically sat his dawdling horse on her rump. The javelina's grotesque snout waved only inches from Ken's oddly bent leg and Dev had lost sight of Pepper. Close up, with its red, beady eyes, the pig was even uglier than it had been from a distance. Devlin forced the stubborn mare between the fallen man and the pig. Yelling and waving his arms he pulled Cinder in a tight circle, driving her at the pig again and again, until the smaller animal, grazed by one of Cinder's hooves, found the opening in the box canyon and made good its escape.

As he watched the pig gather his strays milling aimlessly about in the underbrush, Dev patted Cinder's sweating neck. His hand shook. Thank God for a steady horse, he thought. "I'm sorry I said you were pokey," he murmured, frantically searching the area for Pepper. His heart rate settled the moment he saw her struggling up out of some sagebrush, dusting the seat of her cutoffs.

"You okay?" he asked, riding over and dismounting.

She gave him a sheepish grin. "Only my pride is damaged." She eyed the white Arabian now grazing nearby.

He laughed to calm his nerves. "Oh, is pride what you landed on?" Reaching out, he touched her cheek, needing to assure himself that she was real, that she was safe.

She edged away, motioning toward Ken. "Things just happened so fast. Ken got trapped and the leader charged." Pepper didn't want to think about the ringside seat she'd been afforded of Dev's sweeping rescue. To her mind, he'd looked no less than a white knight swooping in on his gallant steed.

Weak with relief, Dev watched her walk away. She could easily have been injured or even killed, and on the heels of relief came anger at Ruben's friend. But Ken was paying his dues—his right leg was broken, both bones.

"What now, Annie Oakley?" Dev followed Pepper and placed a hand on her shoulder. "West Point didn't cover pig attack."

"Is everyone all right down there?" Rita's unsteady voice echoed along the canyon floor.

"We've got things under control, Rita," Pepper shouted back. For even as he asked her advice, Devlin was fashioning a makeshift splint from mesquite branches and strips of cloth he was ripping from the bottom of his new shirt.

"Thanks, Wade." Ken Boyd stretched out an icy hand, biting back a yelp as Pepper tightened a knot. "Damn lucky for me you aren't really the tenderfoot Ruben made you out to be. Don't know what possessed me to pull such a fool stunt." He gave a short, grim laugh as Pepper tried to help him stand on his good leg.

"Better you than Pepper," Devlin growled, giving a hand.

When they had the rancher upright, leaning heavily on his good leg, he gritted his teeth and said, "Well, there's no fool like an old fool. But Ruben might have told me how it was between you two before I killed myself showing off. Can you get me out?" He winked. "If so, maybe Rita will offer to delay her graduate work and take up nursing again."

Neither Pepper nor Devlin corrected his assumption that they were an item. And getting Ken back to the rim took a great deal of effort. The journey to the clearing was not quite so arduous, but Ken required frequent stops. Rita assumed control and demanded they pause at intervals to allow him adequate rest.

Ruben's team met the weary group as they neared the clearing. His group came in from the south, riding hard, their horses lathered. "We heard a shot. What in hell happened?" The judge's question was terse.

Ken and Rita filled Ruben in. Pepper and Devlin remained tense and silent.

"Of all the fool things," Ruben snorted when talk trailed off. "Pepper, you heard me give the order not to shoot.

Now we'll never entice those damn pigs into the cages. They've probably scattered all over hell's half acre.''

"Lay off her.'' Devlin dismounted, grabbing the reins of Ruben's horse before he reached his sister. "She's had enough to handle.'' Devlin softened his voice in response to the harsh gleam in Ruben's eyes. "It was all your friend Boyd's doing.''

"You and I will discuss what Pepper can and can't handle later, Wade. Right now the important thing is to get Ken to a doctor.''

"How much later, Ruben?'' Pepper, too, slid from her horse. "I don't like the looks of that sky. Maybe Devlin and I will head on to Fort Huachuca. I think both of us have seen enough javelina.''

"You can't leave. That storm is moving in fast. We'll have to scratch our mission today and wait it out. Maybe we'll load up these horses and go back to the ranch. You got a couple of days—Pop said.''

"Ruben, it makes more sense for us to go on to Sierra Vista than back to Larkspur.'' Pepper led the Arabian up the ramp into the horse trailer, depositing her saddle alongside.

"Rubbish! You can't leave and that's final.'' Ruben grabbed her by the arm.

Devlin calmly untied Smedley. The dog bounced between his two friends barking joyously until Dev let him inside the car. "We're ready whenever you are, Pepper.''

"Stay out of this, Wade,'' snapped Ruben. "It doesn't concern you. A city fella like you should be able to drive that yuppie car of hers by yourself. She can drive Ken in his rig, back to my ranch.''

"Pepper?'' Devlin lifted one eyebrow, waiting for her decision. Out of his haven in the driver's seat of the Ferrari, Smedley cocked his head and woofed as Ruben glared.

"You should be thanking Devlin, not harassing him, Ruben. He saved my life today. If we don't make the base before the storm breaks, at least we'll make Bisbee, and Manny will put us up for the night. Take Elena's advice, Ruben—give up matchmaking.''

CHAPTER TEN

Thursday afternoon, Fort Huachuca, Arizona

Rrring.

"General Rivera speaking.

"Oh, Win—glad you called. It's goin' like clockwork . . .

"That's right. Those rascals gotta' get up early to outfox us . . .

"It'll be good seeing you, too. Adios."

Click.

Devlin guided the Ferrari out of the clearing, behind Ken Boyd's carryall. "Rita has more spunk than I thought." He flashed Pepper a grin. "She's really pouring coal on that big rig."

"Didn't you love the way she just took over from Ruben?" Pepper looked smug. "Ruben got quite a surprise when Boyd insisted on her help. And speaking of surprises, greenhorns don't charge javelina, Major. You were brave!"

"Men do strange things when they're confronted by danger. Don't make me out a hero." Devlin snorted. "Brother Ruben wasn't the least bit impressed. And quit calling me Major."

"Oh, Rube will chew on it—then he'll come around. After Mother died, Papa relied a lot on Ruben. The nurturing role went to his head." Pepper shivered, rubbing her bare arms.

Dev's brow furrowed. "We'd better turn off that air conditioner. You're shivering." He tooted the horn as Rita hit the main road and turned right toward Ruben's ranch. Signaling left, Dev reached for the control. "It *is* off." He shot Pepper a look of surprise. "I still feel cold air blowing."

"Both the temperature and the humidity outside have to be at least ninety." Pepper placed a palm over the vent. "Icy. What do you suppose is wrong?"

"You got me. I'm no mechanic. Nor are any of your brothers it seems, including Ruben, despite his lofty claim." Devlin eyed her goose bumps. "Do you want to stop up ahead and put on something more substantial?"

"You don't like my shorts, do you?" she challenged.

He took his time assessing her ragged cutoffs. "Oh, I wouldn't say that exactly," he drawled.

Pepper flushed. "Ah . . . well, I'd like to put on jeans."

Dev smiled to himself. He pulled off the highway when he came to a wide spot in the road. Didn't Pepper know how fetching she looked in jeans?

"I'll get my duffle and it'll only take me a moment. Have you noticed the wind is really beginning to gust? My duffle—Devlin!" Pepper turned to him. "We left our bags at Ruben's."

Dev opened the door and was instantly hit by a blast of hot wind. "There is definitely something wrong with the air in this tin can. Outside it feels like Florida before a hurricane." He moved Smedley aside to search behind the seat. The dog whined, looking mildly perturbed, and nudged Devlin aside, bounding out the open door.

"It must be my punishment for thinking this car was my ticket to freedom. Champagne taste on a beer budget. Right now I'd trade freedom for jeans and a toothbrush. And something to eat." She rummaged around for the greasy paper bag of fiesta leftovers and held it triumphantly aloft.

"Well, we could go back to Ruben's," Dev offered grudgingly. "That'd definitely humble you." Sighing, he accepted a bean-filled tortilla and so did Smedley, who ate his with much greater enthusiasm.

Mouth crammed full, Pepper scrambled out of the car, pausing to study the sky. To the south, faint traces of lightning flashed strobelike against dark, angry-looking clouds.

"No, we'd just be pulled off the road at the checkpoint. We'd be wiser to go on."

Dev faced her. "Who'd pull us off? And why?"

"Desert storms are dangerous. I'm not only talking sheet lightning, which'll split a tree in two or start a forest fire, but when it rains, it dumps. The ground can't absorb the mega-gallon runoff. Underground arroyos flood instantly. Sometimes the road turns into a raging river." She hesitated, allowing a tiny smile. "I didn't mean Ruben. Patrolmen, park personnel, official types—they'll set up barriers closing underpasses. Radio stations run bulletins." She scanned the sky again. "If we leave now, I think we can make a town before it hits, though."

"In other words, we should have listened to Ruben back there?" Devlin watched the wind tangle Pepper's long hair the same way it ruffled Smedley's thick coat. Why was he beginning to think like her brothers, that she needed a keeper? Even more surprising was the fact that he would consider applying for the job. Reaching out, he looped straying strands of hair behind one of her ears and felt the crackle of tension between them.

Pepper shivered, but this time it wasn't because of the cold blasts from a broken air conditioner. Her eyes met his, unsure. Were they about to finish what they'd started earlier at the roundup?

A shaft of lightning splintered the distant horizon. Thunder rumbled, riding on the wake of murky, tumbling clouds. Smedley loped back, crawling into his space in the car, unbidden. Hiding his head beneath his paws, he whined.

"We should have listened to Ruben," Dev repeated, threading his other hand through her hair. His lips hovered a scant inch above hers. "You can't fault your brothers for wanting you safe. You said it yourself—they've always taken care of you."

Pepper watched his lips. "They can just stop," she whispered, edging closer. "Why can't they see I don't need anyone?" She was openly inviting Devlin to kiss her now. She'd been thinking about it ever since Ruben had interrupted the last one. Hesitantly she moved until the fringe of her ragged cutoffs brushed the denim covering his thighs.

"Everyone needs someone, Pepper...." Devlin's lips closed over hers as the truth he'd just discovered drowned in a drumroll of thunder.

Pepper found his kiss commanding and at the same time breathtakingly gentle. As she absorbed it she let her hands rest lightly on his chest. This kiss was different from the others. There was something frightfully possessive about it. She craved more, yet there were things that needed saying first. She pulled her mouth away. "Papa is always dragging eligible officers home to meet me. Grandmother brings home nice men from church. And my brothers...my brothers..." Her sentence trailed off. Just once, she thought, she'd like to prove to all of them that she could look after herself.

Great cymbals of thunder crashed directly overhead. Pepper wedged a space between her body and Dev's, and Dev could see that her eyes were dark with passion. Or with fear. He found himself wanting to keep her safe. "Marry me and I'll take care of you," Devlin breathed as the thunder died away. He felt her stiffen and wondered what had driven him to say that. When had he begun to think in terms of marriage? Had it been lurking in the shadows of his mind since he'd first pictured her in his Virginia farmhouse? Grimly Dev reminded himself that he had no right to make any such offer until he'd cleared his name.

Pepper held her breath from the moment he said *marry me*—waiting for the words of love. Without them, his offer was no different from the guardianship of her brothers. She reached out, touching his cheekbone lightly. "I've heard it said that people say and do strange things during an electrical storm." Her voice quavered, but underneath rose a flicker of firm resistance.

But hadn't his name really always been in the clear? Dev waged an internal battle. It was simply a matter of the army's records being wrong. All around, the sky was growing dark and heavy. Like the foreboding in his heart. "Marry me," he said again, more urgently this time.

Pepper shook her head slowly from side to side, her gaze locked with his. How could she explain wanting to chart the course of her life herself, something he probably took for granted? A man like Dev Wade would never understand.

Devlin grasped her face and held it steady. "It's what your family wants. What my family wants." His voice cracked. What an unchivalrous, inadequate-sounding proposal. Why didn't he tell her that the thought of losing her—the fear, when it came at Miguel's, then later with Boyd and the javelina—had left an emptiness inside him? Because admitting those fears took words of love and trust. Words still buried deep inside him, as yet impossible to find.

Thunder boiled again. Ribbons of sheet lightning skipped beyond a pillar of rock, highlighting ocotillo, prickly pear and razor-sharp aguave on the desert floor below.

"It's not enough. I've tried telling my family before." Pepper's voice struck a new pitch. "You can't marry someone just to make a point, Devlin. It won't show the army or your father that you have integrity. And you don't have to prove anything to me. You can't live your life to please someone else. It's the same thing I've been trying to tell Papa about me. It has to do with the freedom to make your own choices—right or wrong."

Dev's hands slid down her back, then casually linked around her waist. He pulled her slender hips forward slowly until they rested solidly within the warm cradle of his thighs. His eyes glittered dangerously. "What kind of integrity are we talking, Pepper? Personal or professional?"

"A man can't separate the two. I know you believe that, Dev." Firmly Pepper extricated herself from his hold. She turned and climbed into the car, sliding behind the wheel before her weak knees failed her. "The storm is moving closer," she reminded him. "We really need to go." At the same time she told herself nothing had happened, nothing had changed. But she knew that everything had.

Devlin felt overwhelmed by her words and fought his own desire to drag a promise from her this very minute. Pulling the keys from his pants pocket, he dropped them in her lap. Then he bent to kiss her soundly on the lips. "In your ballpark, we'll play by your rules." He'd just offered her everything a man could offer, and he didn't want to think about how she'd turned him down. "We'll get there faster if you drive," he muttered. "You're the one with the lead foot."

Left speechless by his sudden reversal, Pepper was slow to react. She sat there toying with the keys. The man was never predictable. She simply couldn't fathom his motives, couldn't be sure of his feelings. And that was why she'd said no—even knowing she loved him.

Dev climbed into the passenger seat and patted Smedley before buckling in. She just needed time, he told himself. Well, he'd give her time. As for him, he'd had all the time necessary to consider how he really felt about Mary Kathleen Angelina Rivera. More than likely it would take a diplomat to get around both of their well-meaning families in a way that would allow everyone to save face. Dev smiled. He'd never yet run from a challenge.

"What are you smiling about?" Pepper asked, thrusting the key in the ignition. She discovered that loving him brought with it a surfeit of other emotions. Jealousy was one. "Pete was right about you, Devlin Wade. He said someone at the party told him you collect women like boys collect baseball cards."

Dev threw back his head and laughed. "Do you think Pete will be disappointed when he finds out that I didn't even date until I went to the Point?" He crossed his arms comfortably over his chest, shaking his head. "When I was growing up we moved at least once a year. Half the time we lived in foreign countries. The general insisted I learn the language. My mother insisted I learn to play the piano, the clarinet and the trumpet. I drew the line at the violin." He leaned back, grinning. "Do you know how many hours in a day it takes to learn all of those cultural niceties, in addition to regular schoolwork?" When she shook her head, he said, "I thought not. You were probably out flirting with boys while I was cloistered like a monk, learning how to play Brahms in E minor."

"Ha!" Pepper interjected. "Grandmother Rivera insisted Papa send me to an all-girl academy. The nuns whacked your wrists if they caught you talking and whacked your bottom if they caught you talking about boys." Pepper's words trailed off as lightning cracked and spun, illuminating the asphalt ahead of them. Aghast, they watched a ribbon of fire snake toward the ground, then splinter into three shafts and turn upward, lighting the heavens again.

"Damn!" Dev leaned forward to sit on the edge of his seat, small talk forgotten. Smedley howled a protest and Pepper gritted her teeth, mumbling soothing words to the dog.

"That was really close." Dev sounded worried as he turned to seek clarification from Pepper. "Are we heading into this storm, or what?"

"I'm not sure." Pepper reached forward and twisted the radio dial. "No one else seems to be on the road this evening." She paused, listening as static rasped unsteadily on every station. "I'm freezing, Devlin. Wait until I get my hands on Ruben."

The Ferrari broke free of the confining walls of the high pass, leaving Pepper and Dev with a clear view of the chaparral below. Dev gripped the edge of the padded dash with both hands. The view was spectacular. He couldn't remember ever having seen anything like it.

Now they were hovering above the storm that thundered and snarled below. Lightning cut jaggedly through a silver sky swirling and drowning in a sea of black clouds. Spiraling shivers of lightning permitted only a sneak preview of the valley before ricocheting upward above the clouds, creating frame after frame of still-life vignettes. Rain slanted darkly in shimmering torrents, while the trio in the car absorbed it all.

"That is incredible." Devlin's voice was awed; Pepper remained silent. Their hands collided in Smedley's fur and instantly each drew back, feeling the jolt.

Pepper's temples felt pinched and tight. "You won't be half as impressed when we come down off this pinnacle and hit sixty-mile-an-hour torrents of rain." She eased the car to the side of the road and let the engine idle slowly. "Does the storm look like it's moving in this direction to you?" She chewed at her lower lip. "If it is, we'd be better off getting away from this rim."

"I can't tell," Dev answered. The dog buried his head in Dev's shoulder, whimpering at the continuing crash of thunder. "Smedley and I will defer to your expertise, Pepper. We're completely at your mercy."

Suddenly Pepper wasn't sure she wanted the responsibility. That was the difference, she realized, between Devlin and other officers she knew. And it was the difference between Devlin and her brothers. Dev was content to let her take charge now and again. He didn't always have to give orders. Independence—total control of her life—was what she wanted, wasn't it? Pepper decided that would require serious consideration. Meanwhile, someone had to make a decision. Dev had earlier, during the javelina crisis. Now it was her turn.

"We'll never make the base tonight. My brother, Manny, runs a hotel in Bisbee. He'll put us up no matter how late it is. At the foot of this mountain is a cutoff, but the road could be treacherous if it floods. Maybe we should try Douglas instead, even though it's farther away."

"If my vote counts, I cast it for Douglas," Dev muttered. "I'm not sure I'm up to meeting another Rivera brother today."

"Manuel isn't heavy-handed, Dev," Pepper assured him. "Of all my brothers, he's the least likely to mess in my life. Manny is more urbane."

"You win!" Devlin threw up his hands in mock surrender. "Let's get off this hill. That last flash of lightning formed a halo around the car—kind of ominous, I think. If you're tired, I'll drive. Is it any warmer in the driver's seat?"

Pepper put the car in gear, pointing its nose toward the desert floor. "It's no warmer here. But I've got to confess, Devlin . . . I have an ulterior motive for taking the shorter route. I forgot to fill the gas tank in Larkspur."

Dev groaned. "Your brother's hotel sounds better all the time."

Pepper didn't answer. The small car met the force of the storm head-on, and all her energy was channeled into driving.

Dev fiddled with the stations on the radio. Once, he caught the end of a news broadcast. The announcer gave a travel alert in deathlike tones, but didn't say anything Dev and Pepper didn't already know. "It's raining buckets," the man announced. Then he went on to say that only fools would be out on a night like this.

A look passed between them acknowledging that truer words were never spoken. Pepper let out a sigh of relief when static drowned out the useless warnings. Neither spoke as Devlin snapped off the radio.

When they reached the cutoff, the rain seemed to slacken a bit. A swift exchange of nods and the two agreed to take the shorter route. Lightning danced through the solid wall of rain, and thunder echoed around inside the sleek sports car until all occupants, human and animal, were on edge. Three separate hanks of hair and bundles of ragged nerves.

"One mile to Bisbee." Devlin read the sign out loud as it was illuminated by two jagged ribbons of lightning.

"Thank the Lord for small favors," muttered Pepper, her knuckles gleaming white against the black steering wheel. Smedley snuggled into Dev's shoulder again and whined.

"We're almost there, boy," he murmured, patting the dog's shaggy head. "Even Smedley's nose is like an ice cube."

On the heels of his words, the Ferrari's engine sputtered, caught, then sputtered again. Water was running up to the hubcaps now and Pepper paled. She spotted a widening in the road and quickly guided the choking car to it.

A blaze of lightning hit a boulder three feet in front of them and ricocheted skyward. Pepper screamed. Devlin released his seat belt, pulling her forehead against his shoulder.

"I think we're out of gas." Pepper shuddered, letting her whispered words flow into the warmth of Dev's neck.

"Great." He rubbed a sweating palm up and down her back. "That's just great," he muttered again, his lips buried in her fragrant hair. Tiny kisses preceded his proclamation. "Stay here and we float away. Step outside, we get struck by lightning. Some choice. What now, Ms Oakley?"

Pepper pulled out of his arms and wiped a circle in the condensation gathering inside the window. "The hotel really isn't very far from here," she said, straining to see in a brief flicker of light. "That's the old Lavender Pit silver mine. The hotel's named after it."

Devlin stared in the direction she was pointing. "You can't be seriously thinking of trying to make the hotel on foot."

She nodded, reaching for the door handle.

Dev lunged across her lap, jerking the door closed again. "You're crazy. Do you know that?" he shouted. "Crazy." Smedley barked shrilly. "See, even the mutt agrees."

"Devlin." Pepper's tone was a mix of exasperation and hysteria. "I'm telling you. The hotel isn't far away. Listen...the rain's letting up. We can be there in no time at all, safely tucked into warm beds. Do you really want to spend the night in a cold, cramped car?"

Dev cocked his head to listen. Ping-ping-ping—a tattoo of drops in quick succession. It didn't seem to him the rain had slackened, and he could feel the car sway with the force of the water rushing down the road. He glared at her. "Your eardrums must be frozen. It's not letting up."

This time Pepper grasped the door firmly and pushed. "You stay here if you like. Smedley and I are going to the Silveria." Rain blew inside the vehicle, soaking her clothes in seconds. "Come along, Smedley," she ordered, slipping off her seat belt and stepping outside into the rush of water. The dog slithered into her vacant seat, then turned to look helplessly at Dev. A quick staccato burst of lightning dazzled the area around the car.

Pepper's white-knit top clung to her like a second skin. Her hair was already plastered to her head and water ran from her chiseled cheekbones like giant tears.

Disgruntled, Dev opened his door and stepped into the muddy water lapping voraciously around the Ferrari's underpinnings. He felt the water wash over his new boots, molding his pants to his shins as he bent to retrieve the keys from the ignition.

"Damn," he said as rivulets of water ran beneath the collar of his shirt and down his back. He spared another minute to grab a towel from the space behind the seat—the one Smedley had been using for a bed. Then uttering another, more colorful oath, he slammed the door closed and slogged through the water, following the stark white of Pepper's wet top as she forged ahead, bedraggled dog in tow.

Dev caught up to her and slung the towel around her wet shoulders.

"Thank you," she said stiffly, squaring her shoulders and looking down her dripping nose at him. "But it isn't a cold rain, you know. It's warmer out here than inside the car." She sniffed, rubbing water from her upper lip.

"I know that," he said gently, grasping her arm and tugging her along. "It's just that damned shirt is very nearly transparent. I doubt even Manny is urbane enough to overlook his sister standing half-naked in the lobby of his hotel. Must you always be so blasted independent?"

At that, Pepper straightened. She almost laughed, and would have if circumstances had been different. All that struggling with her family, and Devlin thought she was too independent! When another streak of lightning slashed a brilliant hole across an alleyway in front of them, Pepper hunched as close to Devlin as she could get. Calling stridently to the dog, she sloshed faster in the direction of the brightly lit hotel.

Only when they at last reached the Silveria did Pepper become aware of her wet, rumpled appearance. She fell behind Devlin as they mounted the last of the three tiers of steps leading to the hotel lobby, happy to let him lead. Inside the first set of wide oak-and-glass doors, Pepper stopped dead behind a luxuriant potted palm and nudged Devlin toward the registration desk. Smedley dropped gratefully at her feet, seemingly satisfied just to be out of the driving rain.

"Have them ring for Manuel. Ask him to book us two rooms," she whispered, shrinking ever closer to the potted plant and pulling the towel tighter across her bowed shoulders.

Dev wiped water from his face and ran both hands through his dripping hair, then checked his pants pocket to make certain his wallet was intact. There was nothing to be done about his soaking boots and wet pants, so Devlin approached the gleaming antique desk, squishing with each step.

Shivering as she watched him, Pepper huddled against the wall. She could hear the murmur of voices and clinking of glasses that floated from the bar. Wonderful smells of food wafted from the restaurant, making her mouth water. Her growling stomach reminded her none too gently that it lacked food, because she'd been too edgy to eat at the fiesta and they hadn't had a chance—or a place—to stop for a meal since.

Pepper peered between the fronds. Why was Devlin taking so long? Why was he laughing and joking with the man at the desk? It was Frederick, one of Manny's trusted employees. And what was taking her brother so long to get here? She shifted her weight uncomfortably, discovering a puddle on the floor around her boots. She peeked again and Devlin was gone. Rising on tiptoe, she leaned into the plant just as his hand descended on her neck. Pepper shrieked, drawing the attention of a well-dressed couple leaving the restaurant. The look that passed between husband and wife spoke volumes about how disreputable Pepper looked wearing boots, cutoffs and a soaking tank top, draped by a towel. "What are you trying to do," she hissed. "Create a scene? Where's Manny?"

"Gone." Dev shrugged, dangling a key in front of her nose.

"Gone? Gone where?" she asked in a strained voice.

"I didn't ask where," he parroted. "Using your name was enough to get a room. Frederick recognized you through the plant, though how, I don't know—you look like a drowned rat. We both do. But you should be thankful he did. This storm has driven all travelers off the road. We have the only room in town.''

Pepper gazed at the gold key as it swung back and forth in front of her drooping eyelids. ''One key? One room?'' she asked suspiciously.

''One, Pepper,'' Devlin repeated wearily. ''The only room in town. Believe me, I had Frederick check everywhere. Tired as I am, I would have walked another mile to avoid sharing a room with you in your brother's hotel. It can't be helped.'' A lock of hair fell forward, dripping water down his nose.

''The room has a couch and a bed. Or if it would make you happier, I'll go back for a cot. Earlier, you seemed to resent not getting the chance to sow any wild oats. Can't you just think of it as that chance?'' With a gentle hand, Devlin attempted to wipe trickles of water off Pepper's face. ''Could we please go find the room, or do you intend to spend the night hiding in an oversized fern?''

''Which room?'' she returned loftily, trailing fingers nonchalantly down a palm leaf. Now that the prospect of spending the night with Dev was real, she was nervous.

''Top floor. The elevator's over there.'' He tilted his head toward the opposite wall, not daring to tell her Frederick had given them the honeymoon suite.

''I know where the elevator is, Devlin. I can't cross the lobby looking like this.''

''Pepper!'' Dev's tight control snapped. She looked wonderful to him. Tantalizing. Sexy. It made him ache. He fastened one hand on her upper arm, steadily pulling her, towel and all, across the empty lobby. A drooping dog followed.

Pepper's chin came up. Fortunately the elevator was empty and the hallway dim. Snatching the key from Dev's lax fingers, she stalked from the elevator the minute it stopped. She had the door to the room open and was claiming the bathroom by the time Dev and Smedley arrived.

Dev almost slammed the door, but caught it just in time. The way Pepper was acting made him downright angry. Or was the anger because he wanted her so desperately? He unbuttoned his wet shirt and shrugged it off. He was thankful the room was warm, but it was decidedly a bridal chamber. Glancing around, he took in the velvet-flocked wallpaper and enormous four-poster bed draped by a white satin canopy. He rolled his eyes heavenward, wondering how he'd deal with Pepper when she got a look at the hand-stitched wall hanging touting marital bliss.

Quickly Devlin searched the drawers and pulled out a folded blanket. He could hear the splash of water striking tile in the bathroom. He was too tense even to consider showering. Besides, if he didn't douse the light and hide the room, Pepper would kill him. After all, she'd shunned his offer of marriage and had been quite clear about what she thought of her scheming, matchmaking family. In her present frame of mind, she'd probably see this room as evidence of his collusion. Carefully Dev shucked his wetly clinging cotton pants and draped them over the back of a chair to dry. As an afterthought, he snatched the framed needlework from the wall and thrust it face down into the desk drawer.

Smedley had already staked out a warm corner and was licking his matted fur when Devlin slid between the folds of blanket he'd haphazardly thrown across an uncomfortable Queen Anne couch. A very short couch. When Pepper emerged, he'd tell her that he'd actually prefer a night on her collapsible army cot, which of course they'd left behind at Ruben's. But she dallied so long, Dev was asleep, snoring softly by the time she peeked out and tiptoed past, with a too small towel wrapped over her still-damp underwear.

For a long moment, Pepper stared down at Devlin, wishing she was brave enough to wake him and invite him to share her bed. She was sorry she'd been in such a huff, and wished now that she'd suggested calling room service. She'd have to go to bed hungry. She groped her way across the pitch-dark room to slip between lavender-smelling satin sheets. Pepper slept, taking comfort in knowing that Dev was close by. She dreamed of what might have been, had she only had more experience with men. Or more courage.

Devlin was rudely awakened from a sound sleep by a strident pounding in his head. His neck had a permanent crick, compliments of the hard couch. A rough dampness scoured his cheek and chin. Rubbing his face, Dev's hand encountered Smedley's wet tongue. He sat bolt upright. A faint streak of light outlined a single door, and for a moment, Dev couldn't remember where he was. The pounding was coming from outside the room. It took him another moment to realize that someone was knocking at the door. Yawning, he crawled from under his warm blanket. A cold breeze touched his near naked body, forcing him to gather the toasty blanket around bare shoulders. In a state of semiconsciousness, Devlin forgot he was not alone.

He crossed the room, yawning sleepily before throwing open the door. "What do you want?" His jaw went slack. Facing him across a narrow threshold stood a thickset giant of a man with heavy dark brows drawn into a tight V.

"I'm looking for my sister," growled the raven-haired stranger, clutching a wet black hat and dripping raincoat between massive hands. "Mary Kathleen Rivera. Perhaps I have the wrong room."

Devlin froze in place. One hand was riveted to the door-knob. The other had released the blanket and was covering a second yawn. Smedley stood at his side, growling low in his throat. The man's black-clad shoulders filled the door frame. But it was the stiffly starched, wide white collar circling the man's thick neck that drew Devlin's full attention. He shook his head once, then twice to make sure he was awake.

Across the room, Dev could see Pepper curled contentedly in the wide, inviting bed. Damn her, he thought self-righteously. She lay curled on her side, covers slightly askew, looking for all the world as though a lover had just left her bed.

"You have the right room," Dev whispered at last, in a voice rough with sleep. "Perhaps you'd better come in—Father." He made the offer reluctantly, because Dev knew without the slightest doubt that this was not the urbane

Manuel. Throwing wide the door, Dev turned and limped back to his makeshift bed, his back muscles still protesting. Smiling wryly, he sank to the couch, draping himself strategically as he waited impatiently for the scowling padre to cross the threshold and follow.

CHAPTER ELEVEN

Four a.m., Friday, Fort Huachuca, Arizona

Rrrrrrring.

"Hello, General Rivera speaking. (Yawn)

"Aaah . . . Rube . . . What's up?

"You say Pepper and Major Wade left in a storm?

"Manuel is out of town and you called Frank? Rube . . . I swear! Well, I'm glad to hear you admit you've changed your mind about the major—and that you're worried about both of them. Tell 'em next week that you're sorry and let me sleep."

Click.

DEVLIN LEANED HEAVILY against the warped hotel-room door. The time he'd spent with Father Frank only added to his exhaustion. He threw a quick glance in Pepper's direction, deciding it was at least one quirk of fate in his favor that she still lay blissfully lost in sleep, undisturbed by either the light from one dim lamp, or the often heated conversation that had just taken place.

"A priest. Pepper's brother, a priest!" Dev muttered, resting his forehead against the door. Well, Pepper wasn't going to like it, but he'd made a pact involving them both.

Turning, he moved across the room and snapped off the lamp. Smedley, relaxed in his old position near the floor vent, seemed unaffected by the late-night visitor. Nor did he care that the storm still shook with a vengeance outside.

A thin shaft of light from a wrought-iron lantern outside flickered bravely through worn lace curtains like a vanguard in the gusting wind and rain. Its light fell softly on the slender silhouette of the woman curled so trustingly in the four-poster canopy bed.

Blinking, Dev looked at the stiff-backed couch. His back hurt just thinking about molding his long length into those short curves again. Even Smedley's sleeping quarters looked more appealing. As he stretched, his back cracked in protest. He gazed at the broad expanse of unused bed with longing. Pepper hadn't moved a muscle. There was a good chance she wouldn't even notice if he crept quietly under the thick white comforter.

Dev moved forward, halting as the floorboards squeaked. Staring down on Pepper lovingly, he realized the magnitude of the bargain he'd struck for the two of them with the big, austere priest.

Number one, he'd made a promise not to ravish her. But he was so exhausted, he knew that promise wouldn't prove any problem. The kicker was, he'd promised marriage and all the hoopla of a full church wedding for the weekend following their arrival at Fort Huachuca. Little more than a week away. The monumental audacity of his decision settled like lead in his stomach.

Now, hesitating beside her bed, Dev was more certain than ever that he'd chosen unwisely in making the pact and in allowing her to sleep through Father Frank's visit.

Pepper had been quite specific about seeking independence. And what he'd just agreed to do was no less devious than the railroad job her family had undertaken. However, if she'd stop to listen, she would know he wanted her to have the independence she craved. She could work at inventing or not; the choice was hers. And if she didn't want a wine shop and farmhouse in Virginia they would work that out, too, for he viewed marriage as an equal partnership.

Sighing, Dev took the last step on the balls of his feet and slid soundlessly beneath a fluffy quilt. For one tense moment, he lay absolutely still, gazing at the dark folds of the silk canopy, not daring to breathe, yet fearing that the loud gallop of his heart would awaken Pepper. If only the satin cocoon of the canopy overhead was the crystal ball he needed to gauge her reaction. Devlin frowned. A cold sweat broke out on his brow.

Pepper stirred in her sleep. Something moved against his side. A fold of blanket? No, a bath towel, he realized. Dev eased the towel away from his ribs and carefully dropped it on the floor beside the bed.

She settled firmly into her fluffy pillow and her breathing became rhythmic again. Dev blinked with relief.

Lightning splintered jaggedly outside the corner window. The flowers on the wallpaper danced in the ghostly light. He was all too clearly reminded that this was the honeymoon suite. Was it a bad omen? His heart sank. An empty yearning coiled and lodged in his abdomen. The wrath of the storm would be like a summer breeze compared to the wrath Pepper would unleash when she found out how much interfering their two well-meaning fathers had done this time. Not to mention his own contribution. General Rivera had taken it upon himself to post banns in Father Frank's church the day he and Pepper had left Fort Bliss. Testing her cot was only a red herring, something his father had trumped up to bring them together. Now Devlin had thrown in his lot with the fathers and brothers.

A husband for Pepper and a wife for him had been the main goal of both families. So confident were they that Grandmother Rivera had ordered Pepper a dress to match a mantilla passed down through generations. He should be furious with them. He should have refused. He hadn't. Dev conjured up a picture in his mind, and his heart raced. Pepper's flame-red hair would not be dimmed by the creamy lace. She would never be a demure bride. She was all fire. All woman.

He sighed. Father Frank said Dev's parents were planning to arrive at Fort Huachuca by the weekend to prepare a catered feast. Truly, they all had a hand in. And Devlin knew how his mother could organize. Thinking of his mother brought a tender smile. She would love having Pepper for a daughter-in-law.

He sneaked a peek at Pepper's relaxed angelic face. She had become more important to him than the loss of his honor at the Pentagon, more important than his father's reaction to his resignation. And she trusted him, he was sure of it. But would she still, once she found out how quickly he'd succumbed to the families' overt pressure?

Thunder crashed like a ten-pin strike directly overhead. Smedley covered his head with his paws and growled low in his throat.

"Damn and double damn," Devlin swore. Even Mother Nature warned that he'd overstepped his bounds.

Pepper's legs thrashed beneath the covers. She murmured incoherently and shifted under the sheet until her head came to rest upon Devlin's shoulder. Opening one sleepy eye, she mumbled, then her eye closed and she snuggled against his side.

Dev was afraid to turn his head lest the whisper of his cheek against her hair awaken her. Feeling her nestle with such comfortable familiarity tested his integrity as nothing had yet. He hadn't counted on her touching him. What started out a cold sweat suddenly blazed with the heat of desire. Dev stared up at the billowing canopy again and tried desperately to count the lacy folds. He had to think. He needed to make plans. It was absolutely imperative that he produce some logical argument before the cold light of day. But for the life of him, he couldn't come up with one plausible-sounding reason for what he'd done.

He inhaled as Pepper snuggled down, letting the soft inner curve of her delicate foot curl above his left ankle. Had he actually promised Frank he would keep his hands off her? By heaven, he vowed silently, gritting his teeth, he'd keep that promise if it was the last thing he ever did. And it just might be. Devlin sent up a mixed prayer that Father Frank would be the first one notified should he die here like this tonight. Blast his promise—and the man's collar.

Between counting canopy ruffles, Dev ran the gamut of Thou Shalt Nots and was working through the roster of saints when the strain of a long eventful day finally caught up with him. The last thing he remembered before being claimed by sleep was how wonderful it would be to spend every night like this. Locked away from trouble, family and storm, with Pepper curled trustingly at his side. Mary Kathleen Rivera had brought vibrant color to his olive-drab life—a kaleidoscope of hues he couldn't bear to lose. He couldn't start a new phase of his life without her. He had to make her see that.

PEPPER OPENED ONE EYE as was her habit at first waking, and she blinked, growing accustomed to the pale morning light before she opened the other. Her limbs were heavy and warm. She was loath to move and meet the day.

The room was not familiar. Her second eyelid snapped up. A weak sun filtered through lace panels at a corner window, revealing lacy patterns on the wall, along with particles of dust waiting to gather on a gleaming mahogany desk. Pepper was rubbing the sleep from her eyes when everything fell into place and the previous day's events came flooding back.

Yes, there were her cutoffs and white shirt, though not so white anymore, draped over a straight-backed chair along with Devlin's shirt and pants. Smedley was stretched flat on a braided rug in front of a hissing vent. Straining, Pepper could hear the dog's soft whiffles and snores.

The hand scrubbing her eyes moved to smooth back tangled hair. She frowned. Where was Devlin? Last night, she'd paused to watch him sleep. His long legs had fallen over the end of the short couch and she'd wanted to offer him the bed.

Pepper felt heat stain her cheeks. That was it, plain and simple. She'd longed to share her bed with him...longed to share her life. The knowledge rocked her. She fell back against the plump feather pillow, digesting the truth...then almost screamed aloud, barely stifling the cry in time.

Devlin Wade's ruffled dark hair fanned barely inches from her elbow.

Pepper bit her lip. She reached out a hand to touch his cheek, roughened by a night's growth of beard, then drew it quickly back fearing she'd wake him. The comforter had fallen, or been pushed away, exposing his bare torso. Something about the relaxed rise and fall of his naked chest heightened her awareness of him as a man, made her want to stake possession.

Smiling, Pepper allowed herself the rare treat of fantasizing to her heart's content. Oh, she'd admired his well-toned body at the lake, but this was different. Here, in the privacy of a hotel room, in the confining space of a canopy bed, she was free to indulge in the dreams woven throughout the night. She could pretend that Devlin Wade belonged right here in her bed and that he would return again tonight and every night thereafter.

Pepper experienced a tingling in her toes and was properly shocked at the wanton images crowding all sensible thought from her mind. What would he do, she wondered, if suddenly she kissed him awake? Oh, how sinfully delicious it would be to kiss those lips, only to have him slowly come to life and kiss her back.

She shivered. Why did it have to be the prince who kissed the princess awake? Pepper leaned forward, wary of carrying out such a fantasy. Growing adventurous, she trailed one finger lightly through the dark whorls of hair covering his chest. Then, with a feeling of forbidden luxury, she rested her entire palm against the soft hair and the contrasting solid muscle beneath. And as she touched, she remembered. She remembered the night at Caballo Lake, when she had gloried in feeling Dev Wade's limbs against her own. Pepper flinched, remembering how easily he'd drawn away. She lifted her hand from his chest, her fingers curled into her palm.

Dev had been awake for several minutes. He'd been watching Pepper's indecision through slitted eyelids, afraid that if he allowed himself to fully waken, the apparition would dissolve and he would be alone again. It was the sudden reflection of pain in her beautifully expressive eyes that moved him to speak.

"What made you stop touching me?" His question sounded harsh, which wasn't what he'd intended at all. "I like having you touch me," he added in a husky voice. Pepper stared at him. He quickly drew her fingers back to his chest. Her palm was moist. He bit back a groan.

Pepper's hand trembled. Her heart slammed alarmingly against her ribs. She should leave this instant. Everything she had ever been taught told her that. But she didn't want to do what she'd been taught.

"I didn't realize you were awake." Her voice quivered, then bravely gained strength. "I'm lucky you didn't catch me kissing you instead of only touching."

"I'll pretend I'm still asleep in that case. Go right ahead, wake me any way you like." Devlin closed his eyes tight. A tiny smile flirted at the corners of his lips.

"Oh, you," she said, reaching to ruffle his hair lightly. "I'll teach you to laugh at me." Pepper poked him sharply in the ribs. He jackknifed, catching her neatly around the waist. Some part of him was relieved to find her still tangled in the smooth satin of the sheets.

She drew a quick breath before responding to his playfulness, denying for the moment both passion and desire. They tussled in fun until the bed creaked and the canopy rustled loudly overhead.

Calling a truce, they pulled back laughing, out of breath. Pepper held his wrists pinioned to the pillow above his head. Panting from exertion, she claimed victory for her mock win. "Say uncle," she threatened, "or this bed will come tumbling down around your ears." Eyes sparkling with mischief met his.

"Pepper." Her name came out a strangled whisper. "Get up," he choked, fighting arousal. His eyes, when they met hers at close range, were slumberous with desire. The fun was over and the innocence gone.

Recognizing womanly power and giving in to the sudden urge to test it, Pepper tightened her hold on his wrists and smiled a deliberately provocative smile. Equally deliberate, she bent and ran her tongue around his lips. Then, still wanting to tease, she drew slowly back. "Now are you ready to say uncle?" Her voice vibrated, low and throaty.

Their game had started so naturally, so innocently, that Pepper was now unable to realize that Devlin was dead serious. He was also much stronger than she and there was no contest when he broke her hold, flipping her neatly on her back.

"So you want to play rough, do you, lady?" In one motion, he pinned her to the bed and leisurely let her absorb every solid inch of his body from chest to ankle. Dev held both her hands above her head, tightly clamped in one of his. "You're not ready for the big leagues, Pepper," he said, reading the shock in her eyes. "I win. No contest."

Pepper softened at once beneath his onslaught. She melted, accepting the entirety of his weight before changing roles to aggressor again. When Devlin raised his head and tried to pull away, she followed him. He relinquished his hold on her hands, only to have them curve around his neck, binding him firmly to her as she buried her fingers deep in the thickest part of his hair. She'd show him Pepper Rivera could fit into any league, she determined.

Devlin bit back an agonized oath, taking the kiss deeper. In the next moment, Pepper found herself unsure of what he expected. Maybe she *wasn't* ready for his league, she admitted.

He softened the harsh pressure of his kiss. Finding that she was untutored had evoked tender, protective feelings. Feelings he couldn't explain, so he didn't try. But his gentled kiss had quite the opposite effect on Pepper. Her entire body was shaking with desire, clamoring for fulfillment. Instinct was a heady teacher. Closing his eyes, Devlin clamped both arms around her tightly until he felt his own control return. "Come on, Pepper—past time to greet the day."

Pepper's answer was an all-consuming kiss.

"Mary Kate!" Devlin tried to inject reason, tried to slow her down. It did nothing. He turned his head to avoid her lips. "Wait—hold on, you little spitfire." Applying pressure, Dev forced her to stillness. Carefully he pressed her head down to his chest and lightly stroked damp tendrils away from her forehead. For the first time since the game started she let him set the pace.

Tilting her chin, he smiled down at her contentedly. Rubbing his thumb across her lips, he spoke the words that were hammering inside his head, demanding release.

"Mary Kathleen Angelina Rivera, I love you."

"You . . . love m-me?" She stammered and would have protested had he not swallowed her protest with a kiss. Slowly the protest faded to a soft sigh. Pepper wasn't sure she could define love anymore. Or want . . . or need, feelings she'd scoffed at earlier. She understood them now. And she understood something else—independence didn't have to mean being alone. What she'd been seeking was the independence to choose how she would live her life and who she would share it with.

Tension built inside her until she felt ready to explode. She wanted to tell him about these newfound feelings. She wanted to explore them, discuss them. She wanted so much, she was left aching.

Feeling her quiver and sensing her need, knowing he must be the stronger of the two for now, Devlin began to edge away. His heart nearly burst with the pain. "Pepper, I'm sorry. So sorry." He placed a soft kiss on the tip of her nose. "This isn't what I want for you. For us. It's my fault. I let things get out of hand. I should have had sense enough to take it easier." Devlin's voice broke. His muscles strained, keeping her at arm's length.

Pepper heard his apology. Suddenly the cold began to seep in. Had she wanted him so much that she'd dreamed his words of love? Was he saying now that he didn't want her? "I'm fine. I'm fine," she repeated woodenly. "You can let me go now."

"It won't always be like this, I promise," he said, reaching for her again.

"You're right." She scooted away, snatched up a pillow and hugged it to her breasts. "I shouldn't have provoked you. It won't happen again." Though her chin was up and there was fire in her eye, Dev saw the tremor of her lips and frowned.

Grabbing her hand, he linked her fingers with his. "What are you talking about, Pepper? I'm the one trying to apologize."

"I know what you're saying. I haven't been totally cloistered. I understand, Devlin. Men don't always want the
women who arouse their desire."

Devlin burst out laughing. "Oh, Pepper. You have a lot
to learn about me. You were all I wanted that night in the
tent. And the day after at Miguel's. And the day after that
at Ruben's. Your brothers have been more effective than
cold showers."

Pepper burrowed under the quilt, her cheeks beginning to
burn again. "Then I would say it's fortunate for you that
Manny is out of town."

Devlin was reminded sharply of Father Frank. He sat up,
scowling, taking the covers with him. "You shower first,"
he said, abruptly changing the subject. "After, we'll go
downstairs for breakfast. Then we'll talk."

"Talk...talk about what?" Pepper looked confused.
"And shower?" She made a face. "Haven't you checked
out the bath?"

Now it was Dev's turn to look confused. She laughed.
"This is the Silveria Hotel. You know, old-world hospital-
ity. Nostalgia is how Manny bills it. The hotel was built in
1902, during the silver strike. Rustic, you might call it. The
bathtub stands on claw feet and takes a tall step to get in.
The commode still flushes with a pull-chain. You won't find
a shower." She looked around and waved a hand inviting
Dev to do the same. Then she leaned close and whispered
conspiratorially, "This was probably some madam's room.
It's directly over the old saloon. I'd ask Manny, but he
wouldn't tell me."

The smile fled from Devlin's face. His promise to Frank
and the truth of how close he'd come to breaking it moments ago rose to hit him full force. He couldn't have Pepper thinking his intentions toward her were in any way
illicit—and maybe it was time to give her a gentle nudge in
the direction of his real transgression. "Take a closer look
around, Pepper," he urged seriously.

"The bridal suite?" she asked in a hushed tone. "Oh, no!
Devlin!" Pepper ended his name on a higher note. She

wrapped the satin comforter tighter. White satin. White lace. Everywhere she looked her gaze met virginal white.

"This isn't funny, Devlin Wade. What will Manny say when he finds out? If Grandmother Rivera gets wind of this, she'll have us packed off to the altar before you hit the base."

Dev slid off the high bed, unself-conscious in his white briefs. "If you don't beat all!" Stalking to the chair, he yanked on yesterday's trousers, dry but stiff from his hike in the rain. Zipping them with a vengeance that carried over into his icy tone, he demanded bitterly, "Were you still trying to sow those wild oats, Pepper?" Shrugging into his wrinkled shirt, Dev threw her a furious glare. "What is it about the word marriage that makes you run? Or is it commitment?"

"If marriage is such an enviable state, why are you still single?" Pepper bolted upright and glared back.

"Until now, the army owned my life and claimed my allegiance. And if I recall, I asked. You, my lady, declined."

A heavy knock brought Smedley leaping swiftly to his feet. He loped to the door, barking sharply.

"It must be Manny." Pepper arranged the pillows at her back and pulled the covers up before calling, "Come on in, Manny," over the din of the barking dog.

"It's Frank," came the loud reply. "Open up."

Dev turned on his heel and ordered tersely, "Go into the bathroom, Pepper. Take your clothes with you. Frank and I have already met. Father Frank came by earlier, while you were still sleeping. Remember I said we needed to talk?"

Pepper stalled. When Devlin's features took on a stubborn set, she grinned. He looked exasperated and she tried her very best to stifle amusement.

"Come on, have a heart." Dev tried again. "The way things look here your brother will tear me limb from limb."

"Don't you want to see me repent for sowing wild oats, Major?" she mocked, lifting a brow.

Devlin could tell she meant to stay firmly planted in the bed that showed the obvious indentations of his weight on one side. Throwing up his hands, he moved slowly toward the door. By then, Frank had rapped soundly three more times.

Gathering the voluminous folds of the satin comforter around her, Pepper slid off the bed and strolled past Dev on the way to the door, her head tilted regally, her red hair a halo of color against the stark white of the makeshift toga. Throwing open the door in the face of her brother's raised hand, she said reproachfully, "Please, come in, Francisco, before you wake the dead. I'm terribly sorry I wasn't up to greet you earlier."

Dev expected the burly giant to explode. Instead the priest meekly doffed his black hat and stepped inside, shifting nervously from one foot to the other. Frank cast only a brief nod in Dev's direction, and when Pepper slammed the door solidly behind him, she claimed his full attention again.

"Here." Frank thrust an armload of clothing, still bearing store tags, at Pepper. Then seeing she was wrapped in yards of quilted satin, unable to free a hand, he handed them to Devlin instead.

"Ruben called this morning. Said you two left all your things at the ranch. I had Frederick's wife open up her store. She picked out what she thought you'd need to wear." He paused. "I also had someone tow that piece of red metal you call a car to a garage, so the local hoodlums wouldn't strip it down to the chassis. You'd better have a mechanic check the air. Ruben said he yanked the thermostat and spliced wires so you'd get a breeze. I checked her out. Felt plain cold to me."

"Why, thank you, Frank. And remind me to return Ruben's favor sometime—we just about froze to death. What else did Ruben have to say?" Pepper's lips formed a smile, but Devlin noticed she hadn't banked the fire in her eyes or lowered the tilt of her head. Right now he'd lay odds the family was about to be treated to more womanly independence than they'd ever seen. And that was only part of what he loved about her.

"Don't be too hard on Rube—he was worried about you two. In fact he specifically told me to let the Major know his friend in the army called back and said he'd been wrong.

Said a Major Bell went AWOL, taking some general's wife with him. Rube seemed to think you needed to know that.'' Frank shifted uncomfortably as Dev stopped draping things across the room's only chair and shot Pepper a puzzled look. "I only guessed at sizes. Say... why do I have the feeling I interrupted something?'' Frank tucked his hat under one arm and ran a finger around the inside of his starched collar.

"Maybe because you did, Frank." Pepper smiled sweetly. "The major and I were making mad, passionate love.''

Crash! The last hanger Devlin was holding missed the chair and hit the hardwood floor at his feet. Smedley jumped up, yipped and charged across the room to investigate. Dev met Frank eye to eye. For an instant Dev wondered if he should duck.

But Frank rocked back on his heels, laughing jovially. "Come on, Sis, quit clowning around. This man made a promise and I believe him. In fact, I like him. We all like him—Pete, Mike, Ruben, and me. You'll do well to tie the knot with him as soon as possible." Frank rolled his eyes lavishly. "He, on the other hand, has our heartfelt sympathy for having to put up with you, the madcap inventor. Are you sure you know what you're getting into, Wade?''

"Oh, I know about the madcap part anyway. Sometime, remind me to tell you about a frolic in Caballo Lake, an incident with a skunk and a skirmish with a wild pig—not to mention running out of gas in the middle of a thunderstorm. I think Mike might have a valid point, wanting to put her back in a shell.''

"Oh, you men!" Pepper glared first at Devlin, then her brother. "What about me? Not one of you gives me credit for having a brain in my head...and Frank, just what do you mean, 'tie the knot with Devlin soon'?'' She seated herself on the bed with a bounce, swinging one foot angrily. "What knot?''

Frank cleared his throat. Devlin alternated between flushing red and turning white. Each man turned to the other, waiting. Frank looked surprised, but he recovered first. Rolling his hat between large hands, he laid out the families' wedding plans. The same ones he'd discussed earlier with Dev.

Devlin pretended great interest in his bare feet. With a heavy heart, he waited for Pepper to blow up. He should have told her. Now he couldn't look at her.

Pepper paused, inspecting her fingernails. "What will Papa and the rest of you do if we don't follow through with this scheme?" Her voice was icily, wickedly calm.

Devlin swallowed hard, bending swiftly to pick up the fallen hanger. If only he'd spoken of love when he'd proposed marriage, instead of offering to be another protector.

Looking up, Pepper caught the sting of pain reflected in Devlin's eyes. "I'm not saying we won't, mind you." Her eyes sought Devlin's, holding them until she found and recognized the truth staring back at her.

The Padre let his gaze travel swiftly between the two of them. Patting Smedley's shaggy head, Frank grinned and edged toward the door. "I didn't think you would, Sis. The banns are posted and the guest list is out." He had one hand on the doorknob. "This time I approve. Sis, you're in love. I must admit, though, I can't condone blackmail. However, *lessons* would be a different matter. Pop and Gentleman Win did lure you into their snare under the pretense of the army's buying your cot. You might consider letting them sweat a little." Donning his hat, Father Frank opened the door and stepped into the hall.

"By the way—" he stuck his head back inside "—Pete called yesterday. He seems to think you'll murder him if he shows up at your wedding. Something about a Smedley owner shipping out. I don't know what a Smedley is, but I presume you do." He tipped his hat, pulled back and slammed the door. It rocked and vibrated.

Devlin dashed across the room before the door had time to latch. He snatched Pepper off the bed, hugging her tight, heedless of the trailing comforter.

"Say it, darn you," he demanded, kissing her thoroughly, as he whirled her around the floor in a roughly executed two-step.

Breathless, Pepper clasped his beard-roughened face between her palms and laughingly said, "I'm glad Smedley's owner is shipping out."

Devlin shook her. "I'm not talking about keeping Smedley and you know it. I'm not going to let you go until I hear you say, 'Devlin Wade, I love you and I'm going to marry you.'"

Recognizing his name, Smedley joined their dance. The sway of the white satin comforter trailing in Devlin's wake was too great a challenge for the overgrown pup. He pounced, knocking Devlin flat.

Pepper ended up on top of a heap of quilt and dog and Dev. With love and mischief shining from her eyes, she traced one finger along Devlin's lips. He stopped scolding the dog long enough to kiss her finger.

"I want that scruffy mutt," she said softly. "Can we adopt him? He really likes you, Dev, maybe better than he does me."

Dev smiled indulgently. He let his gaze touch her hair, her eyes, her lips, then looked at Smedley. "You drive a hard bargain, woman. I'm still waiting to hear you say you love me." His eyes were dark and anxious.

Pepper hastened to scramble up. She gathered the comforter and returned it to the bed. Then she turned to Devlin, keeping one corner of a satin coverlet clutched in front of her.

"Devlin?" His name came out in a breathless question.

"Yes?" he said, getting to his feet and reaching for her. Swiftly he tumbled her atop the newly made bed.

"Not that." Pepper twisted her head, escaping his lips. Her face flamed the same shade of red as her hair.

"What, then?" he asked. "'You know how to try a man's patience." His teeth nipped her earlobe.

Pepper ducked her chin into her shoulder, neatly avoiding his mouth. "You know what Frank said—about teaching your father and mine a lesson? You have to admit they meddled outrageously, and furthermore, we've let them win."

Devlin bent to nuzzle her neck again. "We're not getting married because they meddled. It's a case of love winning out in spite of their meddling. Don't even think whatever it is you're dreaming up in that inventive mind of yours. Say you love me. You do, you know."

Her tongue slid around his lips, unable to resist his persistent pursuit, and she touched his cheeks, letting Smedley tug the comforter away. "I was only thinking that if the army bought my cot the money would go a long way toward enlarging the supply of wine in *our* wine shop. After all, my cot is a superior product. You said so yourself, Major."

"Pepper," Devlin scolded, trying to capture her lips and hold them steady under his, "I'm waiting! Don't you dare say you want Smedley one more time. And I don't want to talk about your cot. And above all else, don't call me Major!"

"Another thing." She wedged a space between them, flatly ignoring his plea. Slowly her fingers toyed with the buttons on the front of his shirt. "I wonder what your friend Zachary Mankiller will want in exchange for telling me the stories about you that he told Mike?" She feigned thoughtfulness.

Dev's voice rasped in a low growl as the third button on his shirt gave way. He swallowed hard. "We can keep the dog—I really do love animals. I love babies, old ladies and cantankerous redheads. I may even tell you the stories myself. Now just say it, please! I don't even care how meddlesome you get."

"Well," she hedged, kissing a trail from his collarbone to his chin. "I never knew how much I had in common with the Rivera half of the family before this." Pepper followed the trail back to his shoulder again. "Maybe it's in my blood to want a happy-ever-after ending. If you remember, I did save you from a watery grave at least twice on this trip, while you only saved me once. Doesn't that make you mine? Body and soul?"

"That's really stretching the truth, Pepper. Neither time was the water over four feet deep. But I'll give you one and you can fight Frank for my soul. If you want my body, say so, damn it."

Pepper smiled, the half-devilish, half-angelic smile that first drew Devlin into the depths of her sea-green eyes. Life with her would never be dull, he thought. And he could handle another general in his life as a father-in-law. And maybe even a captain, a sheriff, a judge, an urbane tycoon—and a priest—as new brothers, provided he was in Virginia and they weren't. Devlin kissed her possessively.

"Devlin Wade, I love you!" Pepper tugged playfully at his hair. "I think I had a premonition you'd change my life that day you ogled me from the car. Maybe it's why I didn't set the M.P.'s straight."

Dev sighed, contented at last. "Who said I was ogling you? Maybe I was only admiring your car." He fell back on Smedley as she poked him in the ribs. Laughingly he said, "You do know we need to change those vanity plates to read FIRE AND ICE instead of RED HOT—especially if the deal we just struck comes with your brothers as mechanics."

They both laughed as Smedley pounced, landing on all fours in their midst. Their laughter gave way to tender kisses as the wriggling sheepdog nudged them together and woofed his heartiest agreement.

HARLEQUIN
Romance

Coming Next Month

Available in March wherever paperback books are sold, or through Harlequin Reader Service:

In the U.S.
901 Fuhrmann Blvd.
P.O. Box 1397
Buffalo, N.Y. 14240-1397

In Canada
P.O. Box 603
Fort Erie, Ontario
L2A 5X3

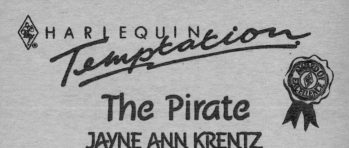

The Pirate
JAYNE ANN KRENTZ

At the heart of every powerful romance story lies a
legend. There are many romantic legends and
countless modern variations on them, but they all
have one thing in common: They are tales of brave,
resourceful women who must gentle and tame the
powerful, passionate men who are their true mates.

The enormous appeal of Jayne Ann Krentz lies in
her ability to create modern-day versions of these
classic romantic myths, and her LADIES AND
LEGENDS trilogy showcases this talent. Believing
that a storyteller who can bring legends to life
deserves special attention, Harlequin has chosen
the first book of the trilogy—THE PIRATE—to
receive our Award of Excellence. Look for it now.

AE-PIR-1A